Two civilized [prey]—[a man, a woman]—
lost in a prime[val wilderness where ma]n is
clothed in bea[uty, and death is a stran]ger!

Three civilized killers—armed with the most
modern weapons corporate millions can buy, fueled
by a blood-lust as ancient as life itself!

ENDANGERED

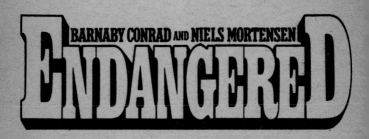

BARNABY CONRAD AND NIELS MORTENSEN
ENDANGERED

A BERKLEY BOOK
published by
BERKLEY PUBLISHING CORPORATION

This Berkley book contains the complete
text of the original hardcover edition.
It has been completely reset in a type face
designed for easy reading, and was printed
from new film.

ENDANGERED

A Berkley Book / published by arrangement with
G. P. Putnam's Sons

PRINTING HISTORY
G. P. Putnam's Sons edition published July 1978
Berkley edition / February 1980

ISBN: 0-425-04298-7

A BERKLEY BOOK® TM 757,375
Berkley Books are published by Berkley Publishing Corporation,
200 Madison Avenue, New York, New York 10016.
PRINTED IN THE UNITED STATES OF AMERICA

For Mary and for
Dorothy—
And for Don Congdon—
Without whom...

"A little too abstract, a little too wise,
It is time for us to kiss the earth again."

Robinson Jeffers

ENDANGERED

Chapter One

Below him, as far as the eye could see, stretched the vastness of the Sespe Sanctuary—condor country—53,000 mineral-laden acres which had been set aside in 1947 for the protection of the nation's few remaining California condors. It was a land of threatening blackish-green mountains and yellow sandstone cliffs and behind them more mountains of varying shades of blue and violet, silhouetted, each in front of another like stage flats. The land was covered with tangled plant life, messy and somehow beautiful.

Actually, as an international wildlife photographer, David Brand knew more about the vegetation of Tanganyika and the Ucayali branch of the Amazon—and Malaysia—than he did about California's. But in his nineteen days here he had learned—with the help of a booklet—the names of most of the growth surrounding him. There was common sage and matted chaparral, yellow yucca plants and twisted manzanita trees, salt bush, laurel, sumac, toyon and ceanothus. Occasionally there were bald spots in the vegetation where a huge mountain had been cut in half a few thousand years ago, and he could see the tipped lateral stripes of ore-filled earth, a reminder that this was earthquake land. Some twisted mountains looked as though they had been slammed together and fused, like prehistoric creatures frozen in the midst of mortal combat or copulation.

The winds up here were powerful enough to blow him to his death on the rocks below, so David Brand had to crouch as he went to the side of the fifty-foot top of his aerie.

He tossed his rolled sleeping bag over the side. It seemed to float in the hot air like a sky diver in a slow-motion movie. Then it hit the first rock, making it jump and tumble till it bounced a last time and lay still, two hundred feet below him.

David took off his felt hat and ran his fingers through the brown hair that was just beginning to go pewter on the sides. He scratched his three-week-old beard.

One more, he thought. One last one.

He picked up his camera with its long lens mounted on the fitted gunstock he'd designed. Dragging the rope and pulley, he backed across the ledge to a camouflaged canvas blind. Crouching behind the shield, he shoved the powerful lens through its hole.

He panned the face of the gorge less than 100 yards across the canyon. By an act of Congress, nobody—not even a forest service naturalist except under extraordinary circumstances—was permitted closer to these cliffs than one ground mile. But now, after several days in his aerie less than 300 feet from the condor's incubation area, he knew every pebble and boulder of this cliff as well as he knew the interior of his darkroom back in Connecticut.

In seconds he had focused on the boulder where photographic and natural history had been made during these past weeks. The rock, like so many of the others around, was made up mostly of petrified sea shells; millions of years ago the Pacific had covered all this land.

It was a flat rock jutting from beneath a boulder that provided a rare kind of protection from the storms common to the area. The occupants of this cave consisted of Nicodemus, his mother and his father. Nick, the pigeon-sized offspring with a huge head and almost naked body, was so ugly that he was wondrous. His large beak, myopic eyes and white fringe encircling a bald pate were an almost exact caricature of old Nicodemus "Nosey" Johnson, David's biology professor at Yale. (He of the speech impediment who used to refer to "the wectum" and drove a class to hysteria while trying to give a serious lecture on rabid rabbits.) The professor's avian counterpart was not beautiful, but in his way he would perhaps play a bigger role in the scientific world than the professor. This bird represented exactly one forty-ninth of the population of California condors that remained on earth. Even without the intrusion of civilization, few condor's eggs survived long enough to hatch. Female condors produced an egg once every other year; and then often the bird would lay on an unnested ledge where the eggs were blown down the cliff by mountain winds. But Nicodemus had made it—and David had been able to record every moment of its hatching. The young bird would remain in the cave for the next five months; David wished he could record every day of its growth.

The mother condor opened its wings, and David quickly adjusted the lens opening. This magazine assignment didn't require any more photographs— he had already shot some 1,152 photos. But the takeoff of a condor was still exciting to watch after all these days—especially with a telephoto lens. It was exciting to think that almost exactly the same creature was flying back when mastodons and sabertooth tigers roamed the earth.

The huge bird with its orange head waddled to the edge of the rock shelf like an oversized turkey buzzard. Then it opened its wings again, testing to see if the morning air had warmed enough to give the necessary updraft for lift-off. The black wings with the white triangular patch underneath opened and kept opening until they stretched an incredible ten feet. Tilting them forward to catch the updraft, the bird was lifted, almost jerked, straight up into the air. Then it slid off the thermal and sailed majestically down the gorge, its black shadow preceding it below on the ground as the bird started a search for carrion.

David swung the lens back to the fledgling condor and focused for the final picture.

"So long, Nicodemus. I hope you make it. You've damn well got to make it!"

He unscrewed the gun mount from the camera and opened the aluminum camera case with the red handle. He snugged the Nikon into the rubber trough and laid the lens alongside the plastic bag containing the thirty-two rolls of exposed film. The filters went in their specially fitted section in the case with the black handle. In addition to the filters, a customized Hasselblad and various lenses, this case contained a .44 Magnum Thompson/Center Contender pistol.

David hated the gun; when he carried it he felt he was just bringing the accident to the scene of some crime. And this was an especially powerful weapon guaranteed to go through anything from a water buffalo to bulletproof glass so fast it hardly had time to transmit much of its energy to the target. Large and heavy, it took up a lot of space he could have used for back-up camera equipment. And, it would only shoot once before it had to be reloaded.

In spite of these reasons he continued to carry it; the gun was a kind of talisman from Elaine, who'd given it to him after an ocelot had mauled him while on assignment in Peru. Ironically, it was she, a cool and retiring housewife living in the suburbia of Connecticut, who had been killed. The gun became a token of their love, their marriage, her ridiculous death, and the kind of wonderful woman she had been.

David took the nylon cord and tied it to the handles of both cases. Then he went back to where he had dropped the sleeping bag and lowered the cases over the side, carefully so they didn't bang against the precipice. When they touched bottom he dropped the line after them.

He would leave the canvas blind up—taking it down might disturb the condor mother and cause her to abandon Nicodemus. And he planned to use it again when he returned to record the bird's progress. He also left a box containing the rest of his tinned goods, canned heat, water, and paperback mysteries.

He checked once more on the end of the rope fitted with a pulley, which was looped around the rock. Then, backing to the edge, he started down the side of the boulder, paying out the rope slowly. He did not look over his shoulder at the drop below him as he walked down the cliff backward a few cautious inches at a time, until there were only ten feet to go. Then, easing up on the rope, he slid more quickly till his feet slammed against the ground.

Twenty years ago no climb had bothered him, but this cliff had gotten to him every time he'd gone up or down. Still breathing hard, he stared up at the overhang with a mixed sense of conquest, fear and affection. And relief.

He unbuckled the belt and untied the nylon cord from the cases. Coiling the line, he placed it in one of the cases, tucked the sleeping bag under one arm, picked up both cases and began the hike down the arroyo.

For the next half hour he worked his way down through the boulders. The ground was a diary of animal prints. He saw the tracks of a very large cat. A coyote skittered away when David surprised him at his carrion. Then he came upon one of the Mountain King snakes sunning on a rock. The snake was almost four feet long, David guessed, and handsome with his mock coral striping of red, white and black. David eased the cases to the ground, but the snake was swallowed by a crevice before he could get a camera out.

David's shirt and jeans were dark with sweat when he finally came to the ranger trail. A mile farther on, the path widened enough to pass for a road, and there he found the Land Rover parked as he'd left it nearly three weeks earlier.

He put the camera cases and sleeping bag near the back of the Rover and paced off twenty-five feet to a brown stone. Lifting it, he retrieved four keys on a ring. This procedure dated back to the time when, as an aspiring photographer, he'd been an assistant to a cameraman shooting winter scenes in the Crazy Mountains in Montana. It was after sunset, snowing heavily, and cold when he and the cameraman returned to the car and discovered that somehow during the day the keys had fallen from the cameraman's pocket into the deep mountain snows. They both suffered frostbite on the forty-mile hike to town; his instructor had to have some toes removed and David learned to hide keys.

Now he returned to the Rover and loaded his gear. He pulled out the Madras jacket and put it on over his shirt to keep from getting chilled.

The Land Rover started on the second try. As he let the engine warm, he looked back up at the peaks like fabric torn jaggedly and pasted against the dustless sky. He took the razor from the glove compartment, gave it a couple of winds and shaved. Almost regretfully he pushed the Rover into gear.

As he did he heard a shot—a distant rifle shot. Then another and another. It was the first man-made noise he'd heard in days. It was startling. Although a long way off, it was still clearly within the sanctuary, where firearms were forbidden. It had required all sorts of red tape for David to get permission to bring in his pistol. Maybe it was the ranger practicing. He felt too good to worry about it.

As the vehicle bounced over the terrain, he felt exultation and fatigue; the job was done. Yet hard to believe that in a few hours he'd be in Santa Barbara and then on a plane to Los Angeles and then east and home.

Tomorrow the darkroom! He couldn't remember looking forward to developing any photos so much in his career.

Soon he was on a narrow dirt road, one that had been formed with vehicles in mind. And he saw

another sign of civilization: CONDOR SANCTU-
ARY.

A yellow metal sign warning trespassers they
would be prosecuted to the full extent of the law and
that all firearms were prohibited.

He found himself humming a tuneless counter-
point to the engine's grumble. His was the kind of a
joy that comes with the feeling of having lucked into
the right combination of time and place and
circumstance that had allowed him to succeed in
what had first appeared to be an impossible task. In
his nineteen days he had obtained photographs that
would demonstrate some easy ways of helping the
birds protect their eggs and help reproduce
themselves. That might keep an anachronistic
species alive through this generation and perhaps
for all time.

He eased the Rover off a drop until he saw the
river spread below. He worked his way along the
edge until he got back to the ford. The water seemed
deeper than when he'd crossed it less than three
weeks ago and he wondered if it had rained up in the
mountains.

He got out of the Rover, stretched his legs and
studied the stream foaming against the boulders. He
swore softly and thought that he ought to get hazard
pay if he was going to have to double as a riverboat
pilot.

Jockeying the four-wheel-drive workhorse until
he headed directly into the stream, he raced the
engine so water would be blown out the muffler and
inched into the river. Almost immediately the front
end dropped into a hole. Wrestling the wheel to the
left, he felt the rear end slew and drop, and for a
second the Rover drifted and the water came up
through the floor. He kicked the RPMs and fought
his way to shallower footing and then it took

another ten minutes to jerk over the river stones
across to the bank. He ground his way up a series of
switchbacks that at last brought him to the top of
the ridge above the ford.

When his car leveled off with a lurch, David's eye
caught sight of a brown bulk lying near a manzanita
bush. An animal, but David couldn't tell what kind.
He stopped the car and walked over to it. It was a
dead doe; it had been cut to ribbons, the head was
bullet-smashed, two of its legs were blown off, and
the flesh had been exploded by a dozen bullets.
Though covered with flies, the deer had been
recently killed, and David looked around half
expecting to see the killer.

Nearby, he saw the site where the assassin had
stood when he fired. On the ground were the ejected
casings of the bullets from a powerful gun. The
shells were four times as big as a .22 casing.

Lord Jesus, David thought. What kind of
monsters would want to do this? And why? Target
practice?

He started to walk back to the car, sick with rage.
It seemed as though this one brutal act had nullified
all these past days he had spent trying to do
something for the condors. He saw a movement
behind a bush near the car. He went over to it, and
there was a fawn standing on wobbly legs, so young
it still had its dried umbilical cord attached and the
white spots on its tan hide.

"Oh shit," David breathed. The fawn was too
young to be frightened and it stumbled toward him.
David picked it up and it didn't struggle.

"Now what do I do with you?" he said. "Poor
little devil." He stroked it. "They should have shot
you while they were at it."

He took it to the car and put it on the front seat. It
sat there, the long legs folded underneath it, the wet

agate eyes looking up at him.

"Damn you. You're a cute little guy and you know it."

He drove carefully along the ridge to the road that led up to the hill and the ranger's cabin which sat perched on a cliff encircled by boulders.

He parked behind the ranger's jeep and got out, still taut with rage at the death of the doe. He picked up the fawn, and as he started up the path a gust of wind blew and he saw something odd: almost hidden behind the cabin a green tarpaulin was stretched over some objects which were well camouflaged with branches, but the wind had blown the tarp up and for a second David saw tires below the canvas. Motorcycles. About eight of them, he guessed.

Motorcycles!

They weren't even the small vehicles made for trails. What in God's name were motorcycles doing up here? The fawn stirred in his arms, and he walked up to the cabin.

Chapter Two

The ranger station gave off a feeling of being both bravely and foolishly misplaced in its niche near the summit of this mountain. Directly in front of the cabin the world dropped away to abysses until other jagged heights rose in the distance and nowhere was there any indication of another human habitation.

Lord, David thought, how important this place—and the few places left like it—are for our sanity. As Stegner had said, "A part of the geography of hope."

Tidily built, the sharp-angled yellow house was at odds with the prehistoric land. It was simultaneously a last outpost and a first intrusion: it might have been a hermit's paradise where man could contemplate the oneness of all that was or had ever been with all that was yet to come; it also exuded a sense of impending bureaucracy, of man's first intrusion into land that was still pristine and real.

High overhead a vapor trail drawn by some invisible jet stitched a white thread across the sky.

David sighed. It was all so damned beautiful; it was all so damned sad. Although only short hours from the Pacific ocean, he could not see it. Nor could he see Santa Barbara, the freeways, the oil spills, derricks in the channel and the oil pumps resembling mechanical grasshoppers that rocked up and down sucking away the last of the earth's ancient energies. Forbidden in the Sespe Sanctuary, these monsters ringed this still breathing land like vultures waiting for the fight to go out; waiting for the condors to become extinct. And all the deer to be shot—like the mother of the fawn in his arms.

He sighed again, opened the door and went in.

The ranger's head snapped up, his steel-rimmed glasses reflected back the light, giving him an Orphan Annie look of surprise. Drawing a quick breath, he said, "Well—well, you're back early, friend!"

"Got a little problem here, Mr. Collins. Mother shot."

The ranger looked at the fawn and frowned. "Man, that's all I need." He got up slowly. "Shoulda left him there."

"He'd have lasted about one day."

"So you want *me* to destroy it. That's what happens, you know."

"If you had a crate I could take it with me—back to Connecticut." How his son Chris would love it! Then he remembered with a pang that Chris was no longer living at home—that he was at the "special" school.

"Against the law," said Collins. He was a nodder; he'd nod after each of his own statements, reinforcing them with at least one bob of his head.

"Do you have to destroy it?" Somehow the fawn had become a symbol to David, a survivor of the Sespe.

"Hell—it'd need special feed, milk, vitamins, lot of care."

David put the fawn down. "Sure it would." He took out his wallet and extracted his last fifty-dollar bill. "Here's something for his food," he said.

Collins took the money, put it in his pants pocket and picked up the fawn. He carried him into the kitchen and came back, saying, "Let him sit quiet for a while in an old dog box I got there. Later I'll give him some milk in a nursing bottle we've used before."

Collins studied David, then eased back in his chair. "Figured you to come back early, fawn or no fawn." He made it sound like an accusation. "Cities do something to a man—fix him so's he can't stand his own company."

David found the remark vaguely irritating. He moved over to a canvas-backed chair and sat down. "I notice you've got some company yourself."

"Who's that?" Collins was continually scratching and touching himself in different parts of his body like a pitcher signaling to his catcher.

David gestured toward the wall of the cabin against which the motorcycles were parked. "The bikes hidden out there under those branches."

"Oh, them?" He looked startled. "Belong to some kind of a club—got permission." He said it uncomfortably. "And those bikes aren't hidden— just got to be covered against the rain, and the tarps got to be weighted down. That's what those branches are for."

He pointed his chin toward David as though to add something else. Then he pushed a report aside and opened the logbook that was sitting on the door resting on two carpenter's sawhorses that was his desk. He ran his finger up the page and smiled his rubber band smile. "You're out two days early, friend. Yet you been up there nineteen days—hell of a lot better than most."

David had never trusted strangers who addressed him as "friend." It was one of the rules of survival that he'd learned from his grandfather.

"Got the job done quick," David said easily. But he found himself resenting the man's attitude—he didn't think of himself as being all that citified. He'd spent big chunks of his forty-two years poking around some of the most remote pockets of this earth. Still, these past couple of weeks had given him an eerie sense of solitary lostness.

Collins finished his notations, stood up and went to a refrigerator. He said in a too-hearty voice, "Bet a beer'd taste good about now!"

David took off his hat with the fishing flies in the band and accepted the can Collins handed him.

"Can't see the city myself," the ranger remarked after he'd returned to his chair and taken a sip from his beer. "Can't see the noise, the crowds, the stink, clatter-crash push-shove fightin' for space to turn around and time to think."

Collins smiled his smile that he intended to be ingratiating and ironed the palms of his hands along the tops of his trousers. David forced a smile in return. He had liked every ranger he'd ever met since he was a boy, but there was something different about this one. There was something plastic about him; his manner was simultaneously aggressive and fawning, and David didn't like him.

Collins sipped his beer again, wiped his thin lips with his wrist and continued. "But now you're rushing away from this God-created bit of earth to go back east to that racket where you got to wait in line to eat at a restaurant where it costs a month's salary to get something they set fire to right in front of your eyes!" He shook his head and said wistfully, "But then I reckon you rich photographers got money to burn. You make more pushing your finger up and down on that little box in a week than I do breaking my back up here for a year. Right? Right!"

David laughed, but it was a bitter sound; he was two jumps away from losing his house and months behind in tuition at the school that cared for his retarded son. The magazine demand for this kind of photography had nearly vanished in the past few years.

"Collins, this is the best job I've had for a long time."

He saw no point in mentioning that in addition to the magazine article, these photographs could provide him the basis for a book. And if it all worked out, his money worries might be over— thanks to Nicodemus the condor and the film in his camera case.

However, Collins was right in that he was anxious to get out of these California wilds and back to the world of reasonable creature comforts. And, by God, a martini at Sardi's would taste good; he pledged himself he'd have one before taking off to his house in Connecticut. And back to Grover, the great old Labrador. Then up the next day to see Chris. The boy would be glad to see him, but he probably wouldn't even realize that his father had been away.

David finished his beer and pushed himself out of his chair. "Gotta be getting back to your noisy civilization and my quiet darkroom. Pushing this finger doesn't do a damned bit of good unless the pictures come out, you know."

The ranger grunted and raised his hand. "Just about slipped my mind, friend. Got a message for you—come in a couple of days back."

He stood up and unpinned a piece of paper from the wall above the two-way radio. He seemed almost reluctant to hand the note to David. "Near slipped my mind altogether."

Scrawled in Collins' schoolboy script the message read: *David Brand, c/o Ranger Station Sespe Sanctuary Calif. Must have pix of you, Condor blind for mag cover. Arrive late Thurs. Wait for me. Paige Evans.*

David was not a quick-tempered man. He read the message twice and then once again. With each reading he felt his pressure rising.

The ranger said, almost happily: "Bad news?"

"She wants me to sit on this godforsaken mountain until Thursday waiting till she gets herself up here for some stupid publicity stunt!"

"Today *is* Thursday."

Somehow he'd lost track of the days of the week. "Thursday?"

"So it seems you aren't going to be stuck up here on this godforsaken mountain so danged long after all."

"Didn't mean it that way, Collins. I like this country. It's just that I had my mind set for going home—know what I mean? And now this damned woman..."

Both men were silent. The trees stirred to the restless winds.

Finally Collins said casually, almost too casually, David thought, "By the way, friend, you didn't happen to see any of them hikers while you were up there?"

David was thinking about Paige Evans; even her name sounded phony. He shook his head in answer to Collins' question.

"Call themselves the Rock Hounds. Got permission to come up here looking for turquoise, agates, amethysts, maybe pieces of petrified wood. Trying to help the handicapped—claim there's a big market in all this hand-made jewelry."

David remembered the deer and it occurred to him that these might be the people that had shot it. Then he remembered the miles of red tape he'd had to go through and all the political clout the magazine had been forced to use to get his special permission to explore the sanctuary. Whoever they were, they most certainly had to have A-1 clearance.

"Collins—could those people have shot the fawn's mother?"

Collins sighed and dropped his forehead into his hands.

"Friend, you wouldn't believe some of the cruelty I seen in my years." Suddenly he slapped his knees and stood up. "How about another beer?"

David looked at his watch and tapped the back of his wrist. As he nodded to Collins, he got up and stared at the topographical map pinned to the wall with all its jagged lines indicating the ridges and the mountains. He looked over at the .30/.30 carbine, the rattlesnake skin, the Smokey the Bear poster and the ranger's cot-bed.

Collins suddenly turned and snapped, "Tell me somethin'. I like birds and deer as well as the next man—probably better than most. But how come you magazine people don't spend as much time and money on humans as you do animals? How come you aren't out doin' an article on, say, how to cure cancer instead of trying to save a bunch of condors that don't have a chance in a thousand of makin' it anyway?"

David didn't answer and Collins went on: "My mother's lying there in Omaha riddled with cancer—what the hell does she care about condors or fawns or whoopin' cranes or whatever. She wants a pill that will make her well!"

"I'm sorry," said David. He was not about to make his ecology speech about all things being important to one another in this world. And Collins' concern for his mother caused him a twinge of guilt for disliking the man for no real reason.

He looked out at the country, down the bit of empty road he could see. Hitching his trousers, he found he had to take his belt up another notch to make them stay on his hips; that was the third notch he'd taken up in these three weeks—and it pleased him. He used to have a swimmer's build, one that got him a scholarship—the only way he could have made it from Big Timber, Montana, to Yale. And he'd stayed lean without much effort until the last few years. After his wife had been killed he'd noticed he'd begun getting soft around the waist, but these past weeks had made him resolve to get back into shape. Regular swimming and tennis were going to be a part of his schedule as soon as he was home. He played tennis better than adequately, but he knew he played like a poor boy and always would; he could get to the ball and make the shot to win the point, but with none of those sweeping-through-the-ball strokes that his contemporaries had learned on the courts at Choate and Hotchkiss and Palm Beach and Martha's Vineyard during the same summer days when he'd been fishing and digging fence post holes and stacking wood in Montana.

The ranger had set a fresh can of beer next to David's chair. Taking a gulp of his own, he said,

"Suppose it must get on a man's nerves—havin' a lady boss and all. But she must have something to own a magazine—"

"A dead uncle is what she's got. He left it to her."

It hadn't, in fact, been left to her, but close enough. Old J. Martell Evans had left his publishing interests split up between his employees and his relatives and somehow Paige Evans and her mother and brother ended up in control.

"Now she's doing her damndest to ruin one of the few decent men's magazines in this country," David said, his voice rising with his temper.

They heard the Chevy pickup only moments before it made the turn into the road that dead-ended at the ranger station. Through the window they saw the passenger door open and a woman dressed in a slack suit and safari hat make the long step from the raised cab to the ground. She turned and lifted a canvas suitcase out, and the car drove away.

When she arrived at the cabin her cheeks were flushed and there were beads of perspiration around her hairline. She set the blue bag on the plank floor and looked at the men. Collins stood up and waited uncomfortably by his desk. David remained seated, watching her. She was prettier than the photos he'd seen of her, and her hair was different.

She was about twenty-six. Her hair was brown with artificial blond streaks and was tied at the back with a dark-green ribbon. Her eyes were a violet-blue under black brows, her cheekbones high, her lips scarlet and too full for her gaunt cheeks. The costume symbolized everything David resented about Ms. Paige Evans: spotless beige with smart though useless belts attached, it was topped off by a flamboyant safari hat, complete with a tuft of badger hair in its band. The elegant handbag on her shoulder was covered with designs that might have been cattle brands concocted by a fey cowboy. David wouldn't put it past her to have gone into the fanciest sporting goods store in town, played Mrs. Ernest Hemingway to the hilt, and requested that they dress her properly. And then charge the whole thing to *The Explorer*.

"I'm sorry I'm late," she said, "but my rented car broke down on that impossible road."

Neither man said anything.

"If that nice young man hadn't happened along with his truck, I don't know what I would have done." Her voice had a dry, chesty quality as though it were difficult for her to unlock her jaw while speaking.

She took a cigarette from a Louis Vuitton case and tapped it on the back of her hand. "Damned fool wouldn't even let me pay for his troubles."

David stood up. "Must come as a rude shock, Miss Evans."

She smiled. "What's that, Mr. Brand?"

"Apparently there are some things money can't buy."

He gestured toward the door. "We'd better get going."

She brushed the hair away from her forehead. "I'll need to freshen up a bit, Mr. Brand." She glanced at the beer can David was still holding and said, "And I am thirsty. I had also hoped to have a bit to eat—I've had nothing since the plane, and that was plastic food at an atrocious hour."

"Tough," David said.

"I beg your pardon?"

"Look, Miss Evans—maybe you own the magazine. But you don't"—he stopped himself before he could add—*"own me and you don't own this part of the country."* "I'm sorry about your"—

he hesitated—"hardships, but if we waste time here it's going to start to get dark—and there's no money in the world that can get us up to that blind after dark."

She inhaled deeply. When she spoke her voice was flat, without emotion. "May I use the hospitality of the Forest Service restroom for a moment?"

"Sure," said Collins, his mouth pulled into a smile.

In a few minutes she was out of the bathroom, the canvas bag had been chucked into the back of the Rover and they were lurching up the road that would take them back to David's blind. Neither spoke, and the silence between them began to build an explosive quality that had almost an identity of its own.

Finally David said, "Look, I suppose I was out of line. I'm sorry about that."

She said nothing for some time.

When she spoke again, her voice was steady, with its eastern boardingschool cadence. "I do indeed wish you would tell me what I did that was so terribly wrong. What caused you to almost snap my head off the moment I appeared at the cabin? Am I that obnoxious? Or are you such a chauvinist that you can't stand the burden of a female publisher?"

David kept his voice calm. "Look, I think I could take your sex or leave it alone—provided you didn't seem hellbent on lousing up one of the best magazines ever to—"

Her voice was flinty: "Lousing up the magazine?"

"Why the hell can't you just let *The Explorer* be what it really is—the best damned magazine of its kind in the world? Just go back to where you came from and let Elliot run the thing the way he's always run it. You take the profits, the credit, all the

publicity that goes with it—and let a professional
editor do the job he knows how to do better than
anybody else in the world. Run a great magazine!"

David was surprised to find himself short of
breath; he had never really been aware of how
keenly he felt about *The Explorer*, nor how deeply
he resented the changes that were occurring.

When she laughed it was a soft, sour sound. "You
are pathetically misinformed. Profits, Mr. Brand,
are something the magazine's got none of. After my
uncle died and all claims were paid, there was little
credit and less cash to keep the magazine afloat. So I
dropped out of school to see what I could do." She
smiled wryly and lighted a cigarette. "What I did
first was—"

"Jesus!" A cougar—a white one. It had crossed
the road only yards ahead of them. David skidded
to a stop, jumped out and ran to the back of the
Land Rover. He opened it, unlocked the camera
case with the black handle. No, that had the pistol
and the wide-angle camera. He opened the other
case, with the red handle, and took out the Nikon
with the telescopic zoom lens.

"Albino!" he shouted as he ran up the road.
"About six months old!"

He'd heard of such a thing but had never actually
seen one.

Running hard, he left the road, turning off where
he'd seen the cougar go. There was a well-worn trail.
Probably leads to water, he thought.

He started down the steep hill, now moving
quietly. He knew there was little danger of attack
from an uncornered cougar, but he didn't want to
spook the animal. He kept his eyes on the trail; this
was rattlesnake country.

In a few moments he saw the river, below him. He
stopped and brought the camera up to his eye,

training the lens down on the bank, panning slowly. The cougar was not visible.

Then something totally out of place caught his attention.

There was a man standing on the far side of the river. He was dressed in a black leather jacket that reminded David of a World War I German pilot. There was an insignia on the back but it was too far away to be legible. The man held a shotgun mounted with a narrow-gauge choke. He was pointing the gun at the sky, and David saw he was aiming at a low flying turkey vulture that was slowly circling the area. Before David could do anything, the shotgun blasted. At this distance David saw the wisp of smoke before he heard the report.

The vulture wavered but kept flying. David wanted to scream, *No, don't—don't!* But the second shot rang out and the bird crumpled in the air and spiraled crazily down to earth.

David watched the man exult. His voice was inaudible over the noise of the river, but David could see the man's lips mouthing: "I got him—I got him!"

You son of a bitch, breathed David.

Quickly he set the lens opening on the camera and clicked off several pictures as the man ran to where the vulture had fallen. At least David could turn in his evidence of the illegal act to the authorities. Why would anyone in his right mind kill a defenseless, protected, carrion-eater? Illegal, an easy shot, an inedible bird—and yet the man appeared proud of himself!

The man gesticulated as he stood over the dead vulture and, incredibly, several men appeared out of the woods and walked down toward the river's edge.

There were seven of them, all dressed in black leather, two with big backpacks. All were armed. It

was a chilling sight, not quite real. They had white
unhealthy faces even at this distance, but the man in
the lead was the most grotesque of all. David
zoomed his lens in on the man's face. He was older
than the rest, perhaps forty-five. Fat but immensely
powerful, he had only one eye, the other was sealed
shut and seemingly without an eyeball. One of his
hands was in a plaster cast. He was not carrying a
rifle, but there was a pistol in his holster. He walked
over to the man standing on the bank. Looking
down, he turned the dead bird over with the toe of
his boot, and the late-afternoon sun glanced orange
off the bloody feathers. The younger man looked up
at the big man, eagerly, like a boy who had done
something clever.

The fat man put out his hand as though he were
going to congratulate the shooter. Then suddenly he
lashed it upward, smashing the plaster-encased
knuckles into the man's throat. The man was
slammed back to the sand. He rolled over and got to
his knees and watched with terror as the fat man
drew his pistol. Then he lurched to his feet and
began backing up, holding out his hands in front of
him, shaking his head in disbelief. The pistol went
off and the man was propelled back as though
jerked by a wire, and then he spun twice on one leg
in an insane ballet and fell forward, his face and
shoulder crashing into the water. He lay in the
stream, his left leg convulsing rhythmically.

The fat man unzipped his fly and began to
urinate. He gestured with the pistol, and a Prussian-
looking man with red spikey hair stepped over to the
fallen man. He drew his pistol and blasted two
bullets into the back of the submerged head. Blood
and bone and gray flesh swirled out into the current
and down the stream. The leg stopped its convul-
sions.

David had been too appalled to do anything. He

had seen a man killed only once before in his life—as a very young photographer for *Life Magazine* covering Hemingway in the Malaga bull ring. Directly in front of him a picador had had his spine snapped like a bread stick after the bull had knocked the man off his horse.

Now he felt ill and powerless. But he lifted his camera to his eye and began to snap off pictures. At least he could do this.

The fat leader gestured to one of the men, who put down his pack and drew a trench spade from it. David moved closer as the man began digging in the sand, shooting close-up after close-up of each of the men's faces. Suddenly his foot dislodged a stone. It rolled down the hill, tearing through the brush. The men whirled and David crouched.

They pointed up, and one shouted to the leader so loudly that David could hear some of the words over the noise of the stream. "Up there, Walker! A camera! He's got a camera."

The fat man raised his pistol, aimed it at David and fired. The bullet hit a rock two feet from David and ricocheted off.

There were more shots, then the men were running along the bank, but David had already traveled far up the trail.

He ran down the road toward the Rover. Paige Evans was sitting on the fender, her Leica around her neck, looking very out of place. David's first thought was to get the pistol from his camera case and blast them—but reason told him he was no match against the armed gang. Getting the photos to the authorities was the only chance.

"What was all the—"

"Don't know," he panted. He snapped open his camera, flipped the film out and put it in his pocket. "Get in the car!"

"But what—"

"Get in!" he commanded.

He slid behind the wheel and started the motor as she got in the other side. The gang would have to backtrack to where the river was shallow enough to be forded, so David and Paige had a few minutes' head start. This road was too narrow to turn around in, and it was five miles ahead to a place where he could, so he would have to back down almost two miles to a side road. Once turned around, he could speed to the ranger's station.

"Crazy thugs," he said. "Killers!"

He jammed the Rover in reverse, twisted around in the seat, and with his head out the window began backing up the narrow road. The first turn was sharp, one wheel went partly off the road, and he heard the girl's sharp intake of breath. He took the next slower, but he tried to make up speed in between curves and it would have been all right except for the gravel. The jeep skidded, dropped sideways and plunged off the edge of the road.

Down and down it went, tipping, sliding sideways. David felt the boulders clanging against the side of the vehicle, and the scrub trees scratching the metal, as he was slammed tight up against the steering wheel.

The cliff went almost straight down to the stream, and the Rover kept plunging for a hundred feet. Somehow it didn't turn over, and because of the thick brush it didn't quite reach the boulders along the stream. Finally, David felt the car come to a stop over on its side, the woman's side.

David gasped for breath. "You all right?"

She moaned. Then, "My arm..."

He climbed through the open window and worked himself around until he could pull her out. Her face was bruised and her lip bleeding. She hugged her upper arm to her. He could hear the shouts of the gang now. He looked around him. The river was only ten yards down through the bush.

He pointed. "Follow it downriver. I'll be up the mountain someplace."

She looked at him numbly.

"They're coming," he said. "To kill us! Tell Collins—tell the ranger. Get going! You've only got a little while before sundown."

He gave her a push and she stumbled toward the river. He went to the back of the Rover and took out his keys.

Yanking open the door, he pulled Paige's blue suitcase out. Then the camera case—the one with the red handle. He glanced back once, in time to see the top of Paige's hair disappear below the level of the sagebrush. Her arm looked all right. She was functioning. As long as she stuck to the river she would get around the bend in a matter of minutes— before they got here. By the time the gang made it this far, it would be too late. She would be far down the river, and hopefully before dark she would get to the ranger.

His camera case was in his left hand. Just closing his fingers around its red grip felt good. He could handle these maniacs, but there was no point in getting the pistol out now and trying to take on all seven here in the open, especially with a single-shot pistol.

He ran up the hill. There was the beginning of an animal trail, but it narrowed out and disappeared. He pulled himself up yard by yard by the sagebrush, holding the suitcase and the camera case awkward-ly.

Fifty feet up the hill he opened Paige's suitcase partially and let the contents dribble out as he climbed. He tossed the empty suitcase under a bush, as though trying to hide it; they would see it. Then he veered off his course to the right.

Soon the Rover was out of sight. The boulders and the brow of the hill hid the road below, but he heard the men yelling to one another as they saw the wreck and crashed through the brush down to it. He could hear the babble of voices, but the only word he could distinguish was "Walker."

Fifty yards above him was a ridge, and running over it was a serpentine trough, cut into the sandstone by rushing water in some ancient time. It was about four feet wide, ten feet deep, thirty feet long, and banked by boulders. And there was no way to get over the ridge except through this chute. He'd never realized the importance of a pass before. He struggled on up the hill toward it.

It took him ten minutes to get to the bottom of the pass. He pulled himself on all fours up the trough, throwing the camera case a few feet ahead of him at a time. He lurched the last yard to the top and dropped down on a pile of shale. He was drenched with sweat, his breath was coming in shudders and his hands were bleeding from hauling himself upward by the sage. But he forced himself to get ready.

Pushing himself up, he took the aluminum case on his lap. It was locked, of course, and the keys—Christ, the keys were back in the car! He took out his Swiss army knife and inserted a blade in the lock. He jiggled and twisted it. Nothing happened. Then he opened the screwdriver blade, inserted it above the lock and pried it up. With a snap the two halves of the case parted. Carefully David lifted the lid so that he could take out the Thompson/Center Contender.

The instant the case was open he knew he had grabbed the wrong one and he felt as though an elevator had dropped from under him. In place of the high-powered pistol was only a photographic gunstock mount surrounded by his film, camera and lenses.

It was a long moment before his heart began pounding against his chest. How in God's name could he have made such a mistake! Some subconscious desire to save the precious film of the condors at the risk of his own life?

He sank back on his heels. Minutes slipped away as he sat there—shoulders slumped forward, chin against his chest.

Then he heard a sound—several noises, in fact, had come from nearby, but a part of him refused to make sense of them. There was a thrashing in the brush below his ledge. Lifting his head warily, he saw someone begin to crawl up the chute.

The shock of danger sent him up and scrambling across the shale to duck behind one of the two boulders that stood guardian at the top of the steep slide. He was panting. How much time had he wasted? How in hell had they gotten here so quickly after the lead he'd gotten on them?

Reaching out, he picked up a hunk of rock and, holding his breath, waited.

He heard scuffles, then a shower of pebbles rattling downhill. Anyone stalking him would be armed and alert. His only chance lay in waiting until the man was close enough, then hurling himself down from behind the boulder to deliver one clublike swing of the rock to the man's head.

With luck he could knock the man out of the way and grab his gun. Then he'd have to claw his way to the top again before the rest realized what had happened and got a chance to shoot him in the back.

It was a hell of a risk. But once he had that gun— any gun—he could hold the pass till dark.

There was another clicking of stones spreading

off downhill, but it was closer this time. David eased farther around the boulder and leaned forward until he was poised over the lip of the ledge.

Then he saw the khaki-clad legs, the back of the khaki jacket with the belts, the mass of blond streaked dark hair. David nearly lost his balance; he grabbed the boulder to keep from sliding down the chute.

"You!" he grunted.

"Help," she cried softly.

She had stopped crawling and lay pressed still against the slide. "Help me, I can't go anymore."

Tossing aside the chunk of shale, he worked his way around the boulder and down the chute. As he came to a stop braced in a seated position above her, he saw her eyes were rimmed with tears.

She sobbed, "I just couldn't anymore, I just couldn't."

"It's all right now. Let's go."

She rocked her head and more tears came to her eyes. "I can't. Don't you understand, I can't anymore."

David felt the anger rise up inside of him. What right did she have to quit up here? What was she going to do, leave them both exposed up here, leave his films to rot on that isolated ledge?

Coldly he said, "You planning on settling down here for a while?"

For a minute more she lay still, then she kicked her toes at the slope and peddled her feet. Through clenched teeth she said, "I am not a quitter!"

"Okay," he said. "Reach up and grab hold of my belt. Now, when I back up one step I'm going to get braced and lean back. Just hold on to my belt and give me all the help you can."

She hung on with both hands and kicked her boots against the hard surface. David worked his way back up the chute, rocking his upper body back and forth with each step. Finally they made it over the lip between the boulders, flopped forward and lay face down on the hot shale.

When they had their breath back, they moved behind the boulder and sat resting with their backs against it. The sky was cloudless and the mountain air had a cruel edge to it as the sun faded. The domes nearest them blocked any view of other mountains. In the gray-green brush below them insects *shrrrrrrred* and chipped; a leaf rustled, somewhere a squirrel chattered, a covey of quail exploded and whirred downhill.

David turned to look at Paige. There was a bruise under one eye, her face was streaked with clay dust, and her clothes were torn from the jagged bushes.

"What the hell are you doing up here?" he said. "You're supposed to be back at the ranger station."

She looked up at him and rubbed the backs of her hands across her forehead. "Couldn't make it. Right around that first corner—waterfall."

David frowned. What the devil was he going to do about her? What chance did either one of them have, weaponless, against that gang?

She reacted to his frown by tugging nervously at her hair. "Maybe we can find another ranger station somewhere close by?"

"Maybe," he said with no conviction, for until today he hadn't seen another person or dwelling in this country.

"Who are they, David? Who in God's name are they?"

"I don't know." He replayed the scene again in his mind, looking for clues, but it came out the same mindless charade: a weirdo shoots a vulture, then six or seven other men execute him. But what was real was that they would now have to execute Brand as not only a witness but as a witness with incriminating photos.

"Will they come after us?" she asked.

"Yes," he said. "They have to."

Paige turned and peered around the boulder and down the trough. "I don't hear them."

"They'll make it, don't worry. They know where we are. But we're in a good spot." A good spot to die, he added silently.

But it could be worse. There was only one way to get at them on this flat place—straight up the trough, and single file. The sun had gone swiftly. It was almost dark, and the gang would not try it in the dark.

"They probably think we have a gun," he said. "They'll have examined the car, busted open my other camera case, seen the pistol and figured I left it because I've got another one with me. They won't try anything until morning."

Nevertheless, he'd have to be alert tonight. He went to his camera case and opened it. He studied it for a moment and then took out three small empty aluminum film containers. He unscrewed their caps, put a pebble in each, and replaced the caps. Taking the roll of tape from its niche in the lid, he taped the three little cans together loosely, then flicked his thumbnail against them. They made a tinny rattle. He found a branch and hung the cases from it with tape. Then he slid partway down the trough and propped the branch waist high across the trench, wedging it against the sides. He scrambled back up the chute to where Paige lay.

A weapon! They couldn't just sit here and be taken and slaughtered by the fat man—what did they call him?—Walker.

But what kind of a weapon could he devise before morning? They'd better get some rest before dawn.

He looked around him and then up over his head.

It occurred to him that the gang might have a helicopter to help them search for their precious stones or whatever in hell they were doing up here. No—that was crazy. But logically, since their motorcycles would be of no use to them now, wouldn't they turn to planes? He could build a fire. That would reinforce their thinking that he had a pistol and was unafraid of attack. He turned to walk along the rock cliff hoping to find a cave, but there wasn't one. The best he could find were some shallow erosions that had filled with debris over the years. He dug to the bottom of the largest in hopes of finding some moisture; it was dry to the bottom.

He sieved through the mess with his fingers, removing the larger stones, which he set in a ring near the cliff wall. Then he collected other debris from the other hollows, placing it in the circle of stones. He found his lighter, snapped it alive and started the fire, nursing the twigs carefully until he was sure the flames would not die out.

He returned to Paige and tried to say it lightly: "Time to come to bed, Miss Evans."

He pulled her to her feet and she grunted with the ache of her stiffness. He helped her across to the fire.

"Not much," he said, "but home."

She stopped abruptly and stood, looking down at the bed of debris and fire. He said, "Go on, get down in there."

She stepped stiffly into the depression and sank down on the soft debris.

He handed his knife to her. He gave the other items to her, too—the pack of cigarettes containing two flattened cigarettes, the match folder, some crumpled papers.

He picked up his jacket and made a sack with the mulch in the center, then spilled the stuff into the depression, some of it over Paige's legs. Then he collected similar batches from crannies along the ledge. David worked methodically until he had gathered all the loose materials he could find and poured them into the depression around and over Paige. Then he slid down beside her and pulled the jacket across their shoulders and scooped handfuls of the materials over his legs and onto his lap.

He reached over her to get the cigarettes, put one in his mouth and lighted it with a twig from the fire. He held it toward her lips with his swollen fingers.

She shook her head.

He took a puff and looked up at the stars, which were coming out in force now, and regretted that he had never learned to navigate by them when he'd taken flying lessons so long ago.

"I once asked an astronomer friend of mine how many stars there were," David mused. "He answered: There are as many stars in the skies as there are grains of sand on all the beaches in all the world."

"Thanks for telling me that," she murmured. "Grateful."

The girl had some fight left in her. David shredded the remains of his cigarette and dropped them on the fire.

"I'm cold," she said.

Quietly he rolled himself up on his side behind her and placed his arm around her.

She shivered and pushed back against him, whispering hoarsely, "Jesus, I'm cold!"

"It's all right," he said. "It'll be all right."

But he was thinking of the morning. He could roll a boulder down the chute when they attacked. He could get away with it once probably. But he needed something to hold them off again and again. He thought about the shale—he wondered if he could use his belt as a kind of sling. Without tools could one devise some kind of a fulcrum that would hurl chunks of sharp shale? All he needed was a weapon that would give him time. . . .

But the long day finally closed in on him and he fell asleep.

Chapter Three

He was awakened by the sound of shots, crisp and amazingly clear reports, drifting upward from down the mountain. There was a pause, then a chain of further shooting.

His stomach, arms and legs cramped convulsively; he lay taut. There was a further scatter of shots. He coughed, trying to bring himself awake.

Without stirring further, he opened his eyes. The cliff wall in front of him was still black with night; the sky was a dark, pre-dawn blue. Without thinking about it, he knew exactly how he'd gotten to where he was. But he didn't believe it. Something was going to happen to prove none of this had ever happened; maybe he was dead.

He rolled back away from Paige, unable to stop a groan as he pushed his way out of the shallow pit.

Paige moaned in her sleep and burrowed deeper into the debris.

On tender hands and knees he crawled across to the edge of the ledge and peered down. The aluminum film cases hung where he had placed them, untouched. The world below him, though still dark, was far brighter than his sheltered ledge; the sun seemed to be rising in the south and lighting the down side of the mountain. Still, in the shadows there wouldn't be enough light to shoot by. Then his parched lips cracked open in a grin.

Now he knew what they were shooting at, and he knew why. They were shooting at their own fears. They must have spent the cold night on the mountain, awake and half awake, not knowing where he was, not knowing when he would strike. They must have set guard, they were too frightened and too cautious to start a fire. Had he been in their position, he wouldn't have built a fire that would have given a gunman a perfect sniping light.

And then, at dawn, some shadow had moved; perhaps a light had changed, and an edgy gunman had fired a shot, then others had jumped and shot, ringing the hills with gunfire. And now none of them was sure where David was, but they would all be certain he was somewhere right down there, firing some of those shots from behind the closest tree or rock.

Still grinning, he eased back from the edge, pushed himself to his feet and walked to where Paige lay sleeping. In the few minutes he'd been gone, the ledge had brightened magically, and it was clearly dawn.

Gently he said, "Come on, Miss Evans, time to go."

She resisted waking for several moments. Then, with surprising control, she pulled herself around,

sat up, hunched her shoulders together in a
squeezing stretch and said, "Most people I spend the
night with call me Paige."

He managed a smile.

"We've got to dream up a surprise for them."

Since they had no weapons it would have to be a
very crude surprise at best.

He looked around the little plateau they were on.
There was a clump of manzanita bushes on one side.

On the other side was a dead tree at the edge of a
sheer drop. It stood against the sky, its two branches
sticking straight out on either side. David broke off
one of its limbs and brought it back. Three inches
thick and four feet long, it was perfect to span the
distance between the two boulders on either side of
the mouth of the gorge. David went back to where a
pile of ochre-colored boulders were. He found the
roundest one, about three feet in diameter. He tried
to lift it but couldn't. He motioned to Paige and with
her help he managed to strain the stone up and with
a great heave, flop it over toward the gorge. Three
more flops and it was at the top of the tobogganlike
chute.

David wiped the sweat out of his eyes and
panted, "Now hold this up here!"

He showed her where the limb was to be
positioned—across the two huge boulders and
about three quarters of the way up the smaller rock.
David got his hands under the boulder, took a deep
breath and heaved it up. It came up and over against
the stick in the right position.

But the stone was too heavy, and when it thudded
against the limb, the wood snapped in two and the
boulder hurtled down the chute. It streaked down
the thirty-foot stone trough, crashed around the
turn at the bottom and disappeared into the brush.
They could hear a tearing sound as it continued

through the sage. Then they heard a shout ring out
far below them and echo faintly against the hills.

David looked at Paige. Without saying anything
he hurried back to the tree, broke off the other
branch and handed it to her. From the pile he chose
a smaller boulder. They flopped it over to the mouth
of the chute. Paige held the stick in place. He lifted
the stone up and leaned it against the stick as
carefully as he could. The limb creaked and bent
under the weight, but it held the boulder from
crashing after the other one.

"Good!"

Then, as though dismissing the stone missile,
David sat in front of his camera case and studied it
with a frown. He took a cigarette from the bent
package and lit it.

The rock trick would hold them one time only
and then only for a short while. He figured he had to
have at least a couple of hours' head start to get to
the ranger's. He needed to stay one move ahead of
that gang—one great move. What was it? *A
Weapon, a weapon!* What did primitive man do
after hurling stones? Spears, fire, slings, bows and
arrows. He'd always been good with his hands—but
what in God's name did he have? A camera, rubber
bands, friction tape, a light meter, a can of lighter
fluid, and where the pistol should have been, the
impotent gunstock mount. And a plastic bag
containing thirty-two rolls of probably the most
valuable bird pictures ever taken.

What else? He felt his pocket. Some coins, a
cigarette lighter, some keys for a house in Connecticut and a beach house in Truro that he might never
see again. The Swiss army knife.

And then suddenly he got it—oh, God, the idea
finally came to him fully formed. It could work—
maybe it could work!

He threw the cigarette away. He took out the

knife his wife had given to him for Christmas six years ago. Silently he blessed her and it. The knife had two conventional blades, one can opener, one leather punch, one scissors blade, and along the spine of the four-inch handle, a miniature saw blade.

He looked over toward Paige to tell her his idea, but she was sitting back against a rock, half-asleep.

"Hey," he called. "I'm going to need you in a few minutes."

She raised her head. Her eyes fluttered open.

"Ever ready," she murmured.

He took out the camera mount. It was about fourteen inches long, nothing more than a piece of wood shaped like a rifle stock without a barrel or trigger. Eight inches from where the butt of the mount hit his shoulder was the long bolt that went through the piece of wood and, when twisted clockwise, screwed into the base and held secure David's cameras. That was all there was to it. David held the mount in his left hand and took the knife in his right. He ran the sharp blade down the center of it, a deep cut. Next he made two more cuts a quarter of an inch on either side. Then, angling the blade, he began prying up the grain, gouging out a V-shaped groove. In a few minutes he had a little trench that ran from the front end of the mount back eight inches to the bolt.

He looked over at Paige. Her head had fallen between her knees as she drowsed.

He went over to the manzanita bushes and found a curved branch. He opened the saw blade on his knife and in a minute he had hacked off the branch. The springy wood was perfect. It was harder to find straight branches, but he managed to cut two twelve-inch pieces about the diameter of his little finger.

He brought the three pieces of wood back to his

camera case and sat cross-legged as he stripped the leaves and twigs from the large branch and cut it down to sixteen inches. He was whittling notches in each end when he heard the crashing in the brush below at the bottom of the rough. He dropped the knife and the stick.

"Paige!" he whispered.

She lifted her head and blinked. David pointed to the right side of the gorge. Then he crouched and ran to the left.

She got up, suddenly alert. She went over to the boulder and took hold of the limb.

David held up five fingers and silently mouthed, "When I show *five!*"

She nodded.

Down below they could hear hushed voices in dispute. But because the chutelike arroyo twisted at the end, David could not see them when he raised his head over the boulder.

Finally a voice, probably the voice of the leader, Walker, boomed out.

"Hey! How about us talkin' man to man. 'Kay?"

David didn't answer.

"No funny business from you," said the voice, "and no funny business from us, 'kay?"

Two huge arms appeared from around a boulder at the bottom of the gorge, the sleeves of the black leather coat shoved back, one of the hands encased in dirty plaster. The wrists turned and the fingers wiggled like a magician's nothing-up-my-sleeves pitch.

" 'Kay?" asked the voice. " 'Kay?"

"One bad move," David called down, trying to sound his toughest and coolest, "and I'm going to drill a large hole in you with this pistol."

" 'Kay, 'kay," the voice placated. Then a head appeared slowly.

It was the ugliest David had ever seen. It wasn't just that the head lacked an eye—it was the zipper-like scar that rode down the scalp like a path across the forehead, through where the eye had been and down the face to one corner of the lips, tugging at the mouth grotesquely on that side. The man's color was that of cigar ash dappled with teardrops of sweat.

"Come on down here! We got a deal for you."

David said nothing. He found himself wondering what this face would look like without the scar.

"Hey now," his rough voice came again. "Hey, photographer! You better come down! Bring the film—all we want is the film—we won't hurt you. You got my word."

David looked at Paige and winked, a wink meant to convey courage, courage he didn't feel. When he looked back the head and hands were gone and the voice was chilling.

"You don't come down, you sonovabitch, we're coming up after you! You won't like what happens to your girlfriend!"

So they had seen her, or her scattered clothes.

David cupped his hands around his mouth. "You come first, Walker—I've got a bullet just for you!"

There was silence. And more silence.

David whispered to Paige, "Stay cool, lady, stay cool."

He went back to the gun mount. He finished the notching in the arched manzanita branch. He opened his camera case. He quickly unclipped the camera's black nylon neck cord and tied it to one notched end of the branch. Then he stretched it tight to arch the branch even more and secured the other end. He cut off the excess cord with his knife. Then he held the branch in his left hand and tested the taut cord with three fingers of his right. The wood bent under his pull and the string twanged as he released it; not a bad excuse for a bow. But there was still so much to be done—*faster, faster!*

Rummaging through the case, he managed to find the roll of friction tape. Holding the bow to the end of the gun mount, he wrapped the tape around and around in a figure-eight pattern. He used half the roll before it held solidly.

He was stripping the branches from the foot-long sticks when he heard the snapping of bushes at the bottom of the gorge.

David prayed. Let it be fat, larded, one-eyed killer Walker!

Paige got up as David put his hand on her shoulder. She moved to her side of the pass; David went to the left and crouched behind the boulder.

The voice of Walker boomed from below: "Come on, Brand—be sensible, hear?"

How did they know his name? Maybe from the rental contract in the glove compartment in the car. Or could Collins have told them about him? It was eerie hearing his name out here in the wilds.

David piled pieces of shale on top of the boulder, placing two on edge to give him a peephole sight down the chute. Almost immediately he saw a pistol snout edge around the corner of the chute. Next he saw the hand and arm appear, then a cautious head. It was one of the younger men, his eyes protruding with fear, his pimpled face white against the brown sandstone.

"Go, Reggie!" a hoarse voice urged.

David glanced over at Paige and held up one finger. He squinted back at Reggie, now crawling up the gorge on all fours. David held up two fingers to Paige. Then three, as he saw Reggie's entire body come in view. The problem was to let the man get into the trough and up as far as possible—

committed—before he recognized the ambush. "That's it," David urged silently. "Keep coming, Reggie boy, keep coming!"

David held up four fingers to Paige. Then he saw that Reggie was gaping straight up at him. The man's mouth dropped as he saw the boulder above him, and at the same instant that he realized his danger, David held up five fingers to Paige and yanked up his side of the limb as she lifted hers.

Reggie saw the stone hurtle down toward him and fell over backward scrambling to get down out of the chute. He almost made it out the bottom, but the boulder banged its way down the trough and caught his legs as he flung himself to one side.

"Oh, Christ!" he screamed, and they could hear the others rushing to help him. "My leg—oh, Christ, my leg! It's broke, I know it's broke!"

David looked over at Paige and held up his hand, the index finger to the thumb.

"The big man?" she asked.

He shook his head. "Reggie. Start piling this stuff up here."

He gathered up some of the shale and rocks and began a wall across the mouth of the pass. As soon as she started to work he picked up his knife and went to the manzanita bush and began sawing at the base of one of the trunks with the serrated blade. He dragged the three-foot-wide bush to the mouth of the chute. Taking the can of lighter fluid from the camera case, he unscrewed the top and sprinkled all the liquid over the leaves. Then he flung the bush down into the chute. It slid nearly halfway down.

Paige was doggedly piling rocks. David sat down and went to work shaping the arrows. When he had them whittled as clean and straight as he could make them, he opened the leather punch of his knife and made a half-inch-deep hole in the end of one of the sticks. Then, holding the knife, he placed the leather punch between two boulders and squeezed them together so they acted as a crude vise. With a third rock he gave the knife a sharp blow that snapped off the leather punch. Two and a half inches long, the narrow piece of steel was triangular and came to a needle-sharp point. He picked it up and wedged the base of it into the hole in one of the sticks. To make it more secure he wrapped some tape around where the metal merged with the wood.

"A great arrow," he said, turning it in his hands. "Except—"

Paige, kneeling, stopped piling the rocks, wiped the sweat from her forehead and said, "Except what?"

"No feathers. Won't fly straight."

She thought for a moment, looking at his camera case. "Paper? Cardboard? Negatives?"

He studied the case. "Good thinking." He took a can of unexposed film, opened it, pulled out a length of film from the spool. He had just flipped open the scissors of his knife and was fashioning the first feather for his arrow when he heard a pistol shot. Then he heard the ricochet and saw Paige fall to one side behind the wall she was building.

Crouching, he ran over to her and dragged her away from the mouth of the gorge. She sat up.

"I'm all right," she said. "Missed me...." He patted her shoulder, then ran to the camera case. In one of the compartments he found a rubber band. He dropped to all fours and scrambled to the side of the arroyo and looked through the peephole. A man, again not Walker, had started up the chute, a gun in his hand, and had almost reached the manzanita bush. He had a little beard, wore a black cap and he was so close David could read the words "The Rock Hounds" on it. Quickly David took out

his lighter, snapped it aflame and doubled the thick
rubber band around the plunger to keep it depressed
and lit. Then, like a grenade, he tossed it down the
gulley.

The improvised grenade hit the leaves that were
saturated with lighter fluid and the branch exploded
into flame. The man fell back yelling in terror and
firing in the air as he slid down the chute.

"Build that wall," David commanded Paige,
"and stay low."

He went back to his arrow. He slid the first
"feather" into its slit. Then he cut two more like it
and put them on either side. It was done.

He opened the small blade and cut a slit in the
other arrow. He snapped the blade off between two
rocks, inserted it and taped it. Then he notched it
and put the three pieces of film at the end.

With the two arrows—one tipped with the
leather punch, the other with the small blade—he
was nearly ready. He went to the peephole and
looked down. The flames had almost died on the
manzanita bush; the next man was probably ready
to make an attack. And they would be prepared for
his fire-and-stone tricks. They knew he had no
pistol, but they would not be prepared for a
crossbow.

David knew he had to find out how it shot. There
would be only those two precious arrows.

He went over to the dead tree and paced off four
yards; he would have to be that close for any
accuracy. He placed the arrow in the groove of the
crossbow, notched it, then cocked it. It took all his
strength to pull the cord back and hook it over the
end of the bolt that protruded through the stock. He
knelt and aimed five feet up the tree. Steadying the
bow with his left hand, he reached under the stock
with his right and twisted the knob of the bolt. It

receded a millimeter with each turn down into the
wood. Suddenly the cord sprang off the bolt and the
arrow twanged off through the air. But though he'd
held low and in the dead center of the tree, the arrow
hurled up three feet higher than he had expected and
to the right so that it missed the tree altogether.

Without breathing he watched the arrow disappear over the rim into the valley below.

Now after all that—after all that—he had only
one arrow! But it was the one with the leather
punch, the deadlier of the two. He would have to
aim three feet lower and one foot to the left of any
target and pray.

"David!" Paige whispered urgently.

He went to her quickly and squinted through the
peephole. The fire was out and there was no one in
the gulch yet, but he heard voices and scuffling from
below.

Paige's wall was three feet high now. David lay
down behind it. He took some pieces of shale and
replaced a rock in the center of the wall with them in
such a way that he had a slit big enough to poke an
arrow through. He took the arrow and placed it in
the groove of the crossbow. Then he cocked it,
drawing the cord back and delicately hooking it
over the minimum bit of bolt so that the arrow
would release with as few turns of the screw as
possible.

He propped himself up on one elbow, shoving
the tip of the arrow through the opening. He sighted
down the arrow and calculated where four yards
would be. Just a bit above the charred skeleton of
the manzanita branch he envisioned the center of his
target.

"Please let it be the fat man!" he breathed.

Someone croaked, "Go, Erich—get him!"

A bristle of red hair, Prussian cut, appeared

cautiously around the end of the gulch; he had been the second man to shoot the vulture-killing victim.

"I'll settle for him," David thought. "Oh yes, I'll settle for No. 2!"

He was calm as he aligned the arrow's point with the target.

Erich had a Luger in his fist. He came into the tunnel cleverly, a foot on either side of the trough's walls, so that if another stone were to be unleashed it would pass harmlessly under him.

The man called Erich glanced up, and when he saw no stone poised, felt secure enough to drop to all fours and begin crawling up the gulley. Obviously he had not spotted the slit in the rock wall, nor the glistening steel tip of the arrow, for he came on up steadily.

But the only target David got from that steep angle was the top of a red head and part of a face that turtled into hunched shoulders. David waited as the man eased up, closer and even closer. Now Erich was stopped by the remnants of the burned tree. He reared back off his hands, grabbed a charred branch and flung it down the gulley. He took a step forward, still upright. Then, suddenly he noticed the glint of the arrowhead and the slit in the rocks.

For a fraction of a second Erich fought to maintain his balance as he brought his pistol up. David sighted the arrow directly at the man's right hip, simultaneously turning the knob of the bolt. One turn did it—thrunggg! The bowstring released as the pistol went off. The bullet smashed into a rock near the slit as the arrow flew through the air. The shaft went to the man's head, the point disappearing just above the cheekbone and under his left eye.

Blood spouted from his face as he uttered a grotesque "Aaark!" The gun went off again and again. And again. He jerked upward, his left hand making a clawing motion toward his eye, but his arm got no higher than his shoulder. A wet stain appeared down his right trouser leg, he weaved back and forth, then pitched forward. The impact when his face hit the stone floor drove the arrow through his head so that the steel point protruded from the red hair in back. David leaped over the wall as the man's lifeless form started to slide down the trench. Skidding down the chute to the slack body, David grabbed his hand, wrenched the pistol from its grip and scrambled back up the trench to the top.

He was breathing hard when he looked at Paige, but he felt good, and the pistol barely trembled in his hand. He had never killed a man before. And yet it was not hard to kill a man, he realized, if you had a reason.

"Did you—" she began hesitantly.

He nodded. He checked the clip of the pistol. There was only one bullet left.

He put the pistol in his belt.

"Come on," he said. "They're going to figure their next move very carefully. Let's get going."

But where? The ranger station was a long hike. And which way was it exactly? Which way was north? Where had the sun come up this morning and which way was it heading now? Even if he could remember that Boy Scout crap about the moss on trees, there were no trees around—not the kind that moss grew on. But there were no big directional options right now. The only way open to them was up—straight up. He worked his tongue against the roof of his mouth and it stayed there; he realized he was beginning to dehydrate badly. Shaking his head firmly, he took the camera case and ran his belt through the handle; he would need both hands for climbing. As they started up the mountain, David turned and offered her his hand.

"No, thanks," she said. "I'll do all right; I won't quit."

Maybe you will do all right after all, he thought.

Chapter Four

An eternity later, David stopped struggling and looked up at the ridge, yellow ochre against a sky of sheetmetal blue. In the unpolluted air the mountain appeared near enough to be leaning down against them. The sun seemed to burn through his hat and skull and more and more frequently the peaks went out of focus and rippled as though seen through an invisible river.

The climb past boulders and through scrub and manzanita had torn his hands, arms and legs; his trousers were ripped in a dozen places. Paige had sagged to the ground.

His lips worked dryly, making a clicking sound against each other, his swollen tongue ached when he pushed it against his teeth. As he looked, the ridge above him miraculously became covered with

snow—glacial snow no more than a few hundred
yards above him. He shook his head and looked
again and there was no snow; only shale blazing in
the afternoon sun.

His jacket that had earlier been drenched with
sweat was again dry; all the fluid had been sucked
out of him.

Water! He desperately needed water. Without
thinking he said the word aloud, "Waa-er," but the
sound that came from his throat was unintelliglble.

Paige twisted her head to peer up at him. She
blinked.

"Up," he said.

They struggled together like drunken mario-
nettes until she was standing; then again they
pushed upward.

Fragments of a half-remembered poem swirled
through his head as they slipped and staggered up
the hot incline.

> *Wind has mountains;*
> *cliffs of fall*
> *Frightful, sheet*
> *no-man-fathomed.*

And they kept going one step at a time. A step.
Another. A step. Slip. Stagger, balance, a step—
damnit foot, a step!

Suddenly Paige slipped, pitched, fell. And she lay
there, her stomach barely moving with her breath.
She closed her eyes against the ravaging sun, her lips
worked soundlessly for a minute. Then, hoarsely,
"Sorry."

He sat down beside her so his shadow gave her
shade. How was this going to end? An hour earlier
they had passed a cougar kill—a ripped doe. Was
that how it was going to be for them? He thought of

Elaine; he'd never believed in afterlife, but now he saw her clearly up there in the cloudless sky. She was watching them, unable to help, her smile quite sad and disapproving as she saw them dying there on the mountain.

Maybe she'd been right all along; maybe he should have settled down to some stable job like everybody else.

He jostled Paige till she woke. "Now," he said, "now we're gonna make it. Gonna make it."

She sighed, and at his prodding lifted her arms about his neck; he rolled over on his hands and knees below her and locked her hands beneath his chin. Using the steepness of the hill to his advantage, he pressed to his feet, boosting her on his back and tottered back a number of steps until he caught his balance, then strained upward again, his calves knotting in pain from the double burden.

A mournful melody kept intruding into his brain, over and over it sang. He tried to think what it was. At last it came to him. It was a favorite of Elaine's— was it by Satie? He kept his head down, concentrating on the steep pocked ground and the music, not thinking about whether they would make it.

And then he came to the end. It was a wall of loose shale spilling down between two rock cliffs as abrupt as a ladder set against the side of a building. He swayed forward and sank to his hands and knees, then down to lie on the baking earth. Paige groaned as she rolled off him. He lay there, sucking great breaths of air into his seared lungs.

And then the earth took on a reddish haze. He went mad, wild with a terrible anger. He beat the hot boulders with the heels of his hands and pounded the earth with his madness.

Standing up with the energy of his fury, he went to the base of the slide and kicked insanely at the loose rock. The slide was at least a hundred feet high, perhaps more. God knew where it started. God only knew if the cliffs formed a ledge above.

He turned and looked at the world spread out below him. He would not give up the heights he'd fought so desperately to win. There was no way around the cliffs, and they were sheer—ropes and crampons and pitons and experience and fresh energy might scale them; he and the girl had none of the qualifications.

He sat, folded his arms across his knees, dropped his head in frustration. And then, in his madness, he saw how it could be done; very clearly he saw them doing it. They would lie face down on that hot, jagged rubble, and they would crawl up it. One mini-step, one mini-pull at a time. Paige would go first. He would put his hands under the soles of her shoes, each time she moved her foot up even two inches he would get his hand up and help press her toe into the shale to give her purchase to take the next step with her other foot. And once her feet were secured, he could pull himself up those inches too.

He stamped back down to where Paige lay asleep. "Let's go!"

Her eyes moved behind her still closed lids. "Tired," she whispered.

He bent over and slapped the side of her face, hard once, gritted his teeth and slapped it hard again. Her eyes snapped open; she rocked up on her elbows, her teeth bared at him.

She lunged to her feet, stamped awkwardly, legs apart, to the base of the slide where the rubble dished out. She continued stamping till she fell face forward against the almost vertical slope. And still she kicked her feet.

David scrambled behind her, caught her right

heel in his palm and pressed it into the mass of pebbles.

"Okay, lady," he grunted. "That's one."

Her left leg kicked futilely a time or two, shooting stones and dirt down on his head; then she lay still for a moment before she pressed down on her right foot and moved up six inches.

David pulled himself up beneath her and pinioned the left foot. He coughed, then, "Two." And she moved up again.

And by ones and by twos and by ones and slides back, losing yards they had only just earned by inches, they wormed their way up the steep purgatory, losing sense of time, of count, of self. There was only the present "One" and the inexorable "Two."

Neither ever remembered climbing over the top of the ridge. He lay there heaving for a long time, it seemed, Paige crumpled near him.

Finally he sat up. "Okay?"

"All right," she said, barely audibly.

It was best to level with her. "Paige," he said, "I haven't the damndest idea in hell where we are. The ranger station could be anyplace"—he swung his arm slowly in a three-hundred-and-sixty-degree circle—"any damned place. I couldn't see any lights last night; this morning the sun seemed to be rising in the south."

Quietly she said, "You mean we're lost—really lost!"

"Really lost. And they're going to be coming after us soon. They've got to get that film. And they've got to get us. Unless they figure this country will get us."

Now she thought about it. "So—so then?"

"I can't help but think that Collins knows we are

lost. He must have expected us last night. Perhaps he thinks we spent the night at the condor blind. But today, tomorrow at the latest, he must become worried. He'll send someone looking for us."

"Today—" she said. "Or tomorrow."

"Tomorrow, for sure."

"Except," she said, "he looked like an incompetent son of a bitch to me."

He took a deep breath, straightened and slapped his hands down on his knees. "I hope you're wrong. But it doesn't matter about Collins. We're going to make it. We're going to stay inside the shadows. We're going to damned well find water down there. And we're going to ease west. We're bound to come out somewhere if we just keep going west. Right? Right!"

She nodded as though agreeing with him, but said, "I think west is over that way." She pointed in a direction almost at right angles to where David sensed west should be.

He scowled, more uncertain of himself than before. He glanced at his watch and was surprised to find it was a little past three o'clock. Because of the towering mountains, it was impossible to get a feeling of where the actual horizon was or how high the sun.

Kneeling, he found a bit of ground that appeared level and brushed it clear with his hand. Then he removed his watch and laid it face up on the spot he'd cleared. He selected a pine needle from the debris he'd pushed aside, set one end on the ground near the watch and held the other end with his thumb and index finger so that it stood vertical. With his other hand he twisted the watch until the slender shadow fell directly along the shorter hour hand pointing just past the three mark.

Paige watched these mysterious operations with

growing curiosity. "What're you doing with all that?"

"Works like a compass," he said. "Crude, but close enough."

She frowned. "So how do you tell which way is west?"

"Well, south is halfway between the hour hand that's pointing at the sun and the twelve o'clock position—let's say, about one thirty." He calculated ninety degrees on the watch face, and said, "So west would be a touch past ten-thirty, or—that way."

She looked in the direction he pointed. "You mean we were both wrong? Are you sure?"

"Give or take eight degrees," he said as he stood and refastened the watch to his wrist.

"You *were* a Boy Scout." She said it almost as an accusation.

He shook his head. "Grew up on a ranch in the wilds of Montana."

He collected the gun, the knife, the roll of film of the murder, the odds and ends, and distributed them—some for his pants pockets, some for the jacket.

He picked up the camera case with the condor films that had caused this predicament and started climbing to the ridge.

Suddenly Paige said, "Does it make sense to burden yourself with that damned camera case?"

He hesitated. No point in telling her that besides just an article for her magazine those films represented hope for the condors' long-range survival—and, with the money a book made of them would bring, the immediate survival of David Brand, his home and his son.

"Yes," he said. "It does."

Whereas the ascent on the westerly side of the mountain had been arduous, the descent from the north rim was treacherous. Leading the way to explore broken-off cliffs and vertical chimneys, David suffered two jarring falls in the first hour. The second time he cut his hand deeply on a jagged outcropping. Paige managed to scramble past the point that had given way under him, then she helped cut a strip of cloth from his jacket and bound the wound. Another cautious hour brought them to a saddle ridge.

Now he guessed they were headed due east. But he thought he had seen a flickering snake of a river in a distant gorge. They would rest and then push hard for the river.

Hoarsely he said, "Rest," and slumped to the ground. Paige staggered to where he sat and sagged next to him, coming down almost as though the bones were gone from her body; she lay on her back, panting dryly.

He hunched forward and stared out at the distance again. A bird hovered somewhere above the next bluff. At first he thought it was a buzzard, a turkey vulture—perhaps the first of many scavengers instinctively coming to seek out signs of their impending death. Then he caught a sharp look at its silhouette. He saw the shorter tail, the glint of an orange head and the white linings under the ten-foot wingspread: a condor!

He made a noise that was halfway between a laugh and a sob. Here was one of his friends, the great creatures that had gotten them into this mess; he thought of how worried the magazine had been so long ago that he would never see one. And here one of the fabled birds had come looking for him.

Did this mean that they were close to the blind where he had photographed them? But it didn't look at all like the same terrain, and he reminded himself that the creatures easily ranged ten miles in a morning's flight.

The bird tilted its wings and began to sail away.

"Condor," he said to Paige.

She wasn't looking at the bird but down the mountain and across the valley beyond the river. "Look!" she whispered. "Look!"

It was a light, a bright light that comes from sun glancing off glass. And where there was glass there were sure to be humans. The fear flashed through David's mind that they'd come to the gang's hideout. But Collins had said they'd only been around for the past couple of days—hardly time to build a house.

"Come on!" David said, his hopes rising.

He got up and pulled her with him. They stumbled down the rocks for two more hours. Then, abruptly, the boulders parted to an animal trail which led into pine trees. There were paw prints on the trail, big ones—a mountain lion's. He could no longer see the river or the reflected light because of the trees.

"Wait," he panted. He put down the case. He left the trail and climbed up to a cluster of boulders set back in the pines. He passed the opening of a cave, almost hidden by the branches of a tree. It was a large cave, the kind of a shelter they should have had the evening before. He looked in to see if any makers of the paw prints were in residence. It was empty. Scrambling up the boulders that made up the mouth of the cave, he crawled out onto a ledge and stood up so that he could see above the trees. They were on course toward the light that now in the late afternoon sun looked as though it were glancing off a large windowpane. It was just across the river, which lay straight ahead not more than a mile away.

He climbed back down and hurried to the trail. Paige was not there. He thought immediately of the cougar and bear tracks. Then she appeared up ahead of him. He was surprised at how relieved he was to see her.

"Had to go," she explained. Then she whispered: "David—I thought I saw someone—down there! A few moments ago!"

Lord, they've caught up. "What'd they look like—how many?"

"Just one—I'm not even sure it was a man. Just a glimpse, a body—then it was gone."

"Probably some animal," he said. But he felt the pistol in his pocket with its one bullet. "Just an animal."

They walked quickly toward the river. They could hear its roar now. Then suddenly they came upon it, frothy with its rush down the mountain. They flung themselves to the ground and hung down headfirst over the bank and splashed water into their mouths and onto their faces and behind their necks. David filled his hat with water and dumped it over his head.

"Don't drink too much," David gasped. He looked across the river at the woods. In there, not a thousand yards away, had to be the dwelling whose panes of glass were reflecting the light. Who would be living out here—who would build a house out here in nothingness? It would certainly not be a ranger lookout hunkered down here in a forest. He would settle for anyone who would give them food and shelter. God, he was hungry and bruised and stiff, and he knew Paige couldn't go on much longer.

But how to get across this deep ten yards of rushing water? Maybe there was a solution to the problem, but he was too beat to figure it out now.

The light of the evening sun would not last long either.

"We'd better settle down here for the night," he said, getting up.

He saw the line of disappointment come between her eyebrows and she lay back on the bank.

"I know," he said. "I was counting on that house too. But I'll figure a way to get across tomorrow. You must be starved."

"It's not so bad," she said. "Not with the water in me."

He looked around him. "We'll go back in the trees." He thought of the cave.

"Come on." He put out his hand and pulled her up.

They went back up to the cave. David went in, but Paige hung back.

"Come in—it's all right."

It was deep and dark in back. David lit a match. There were some animal droppings, but the floor was smooth, and the rock walls and ceiling were dry. He put down his camera case.

"It'll do fine," he said. "Better than last night." Then: "Paige—if you're up to it—"

"I'm up to it."

"Good. Gather a bunch of leaves and twigs—find some dead branches. See if you can start a fire. We're safe here. I'll see if I can't get something to eat."

He handed her the matches and left the cave, heading down to the river to where the water wasn't so swift. Part of the stream split off and formed a quiet pool. Cautiously David walked toward it. He saw a dark shape dart across the pool and then another zigzagged behind it, and another.

He sat down on the bank, took off his hat, and

worked one of the artificial flies out of the band, the Adams with a few inches of transparent leader still attached. He pulled the leather shoelace out of one of his boots and threaded the end of the leader into the loop, twisted it around the thong several times in the standard fisherman's knot, and pulled it tight. He went to a large sumac bush and cut off a five-foot branch. After stripping off the leaves, he tied the thong to the tip. Then, on all fours so that he wouldn't vibrate the bank and alert the fish, he stalked the far end of the pool. Cautiously he reached out, extending his rod out over the water and lowering the fly into the swirl. Damn—the thong looked like a hawser, so thick and dark against the water. If only he had a couple of feet of the transparent leader instead of a few inches. But the fly rode the water in a natural enough fashion down and across the pool.

A greenish-silver shape—a good-sized trout—suddenly materialized under the fly and studied it.

"Come on, come on," David urged silently, as the rainbow hesitated. "Take it!"

The fish moved closer, looked as though it might strike at it, then apparently spooked by the shoelace, it suddenly whirled and was gone.

"Damn, damn!"

David cast several more times but no other fish appeared. It was growing darker and there was no more time for subtleties. He would have to try a more primitive method, the way he'd seen the natives in Fiji do it.

He replaced the shoelace in his boot then cut two leafy branches from the sumac bush. With one in each hand he stepped into the water up to his knees. Even in the shallows the torrent was so strong he had to fight to keep his balance as he waded down the center of the pool, beating the river on each side of him with the branches. He saw the dark shapes darting in front of him as he splashed his way toward a gravel bar that jutted out from the bank. Soon the water shallowed out to a foot, then to inches. A half dozen trout were trapped among the rocks in front of him. He flung away the branches, dropped to his knees and began grabbing at the fish. He caught the largest one in both hands and lifted it out of the water, but it spurted from his fingers like a banana out of its skin and thrashed away into deeper water. The next one he got his hands on he flipped out of the water onto the gravel and before it could flop back into the stream he dug his thumb and forefinger into its gills and hung on. Then, with his left hand he managed to gill another smaller one before all the other fish worked their way into deeper water.

He waded ashore, his legs numb from the cold water. The sun was gone now and he had difficulty finding the path in the gloom.

When he was in the vicinity of the cave he called out "Paige!" several times. Finally she answered and he followed the sound to the cave. Only then could he see the fire she had built.

"I was getting worried," she said. "You're drenched."

"Worth it," he replied. He laid the fish, one of which weighed at least a pound and a half, on a rock. She not only had built a big fire but had stacked a pile of branches and twigs against the wall. "You've been busy. Good girl."

"I'm trying to cope. My father always said, 'You've got to cope, girl!' He loved English girls— lots of them—and he was always droning on about how they can cope with anything."

David took off his boots and socks and put them

by the fire. Then he took the knife out of his pocket, slid off the wet trousers and draped them over a boulder.

"I never thought a fish would look so good," Paige said as he picked up the larger rainbow. He slit it up the belly and at the gills, inserted his middle finger at the bottom and his thumb at the top of the incision, and stripped out the entrails in one motion. He started to throw them out of the cave, then thought of the animals and tossed them on the fire. The smell of the searing flesh stung his nostrils and smelled good as he cleaned the other trout.

"Do you like to cook?" he asked.

She sighed. "Under duress I might be able to scramble an egg. I'm afraid I was too busy being a tomboy to learn when I was young. Horses were my life. I only got off a horse long enough to go to horse shows."

"I'm so hungry I could eat it raw."

He went outside, cut a branch off the tree and began whittling off the leaves. When he came back in, Paige was stretching his wet pants over a makeshift rack of sticks propped against a boulder near the fire.

"Valet service," she said. "I'm coping."

"It's appreciated." Inserting the point of the branch through the fish's mouth, he shoved it the length of the body. Then he held the spitted fish over the fire. He turned it slowly and the trout's skin soon went dark, wrinkled, and split with the heat as they watched. When the fish no longer turned with the stick, David took it away from the flame, and put it on his battered camera case and filleted it skillfully.

"Dinner," he announced, "is served."

Paige took some of the pink flesh with her fingers eagerly.

"Eat up, lady, eat up," said David.

"You too," she replied with her mouth full. "Delicious! You must have been the best Boy Scout in the troop."

"I told you, a Boy Scout I never was."

"What were you like," she said between mouthfuls, "when you were a little boy?"

He didn't like this nostalgia game. At least, not with other people. "I was born with the gift of laughter," he said lightly, "and a sense that the world was mad."

"Sabatini," she said, licking her fingers.

He was impressed.

"That's an old book," he said. "How'd you know it?"

"When I wasn't on a horse I had my nose in a book."

For a moment he let himself go back to those books in his father's den—he could still hear his father's voice already hoarse with the cancer that would kill him, reading to him from the books that would early on instill in him a craving for adventure. Sabatini. And Kipling. *Something hidden. Go and find it. Go and look behind the ranges—something lost behind the ranges. Lost and waiting for you. Go!*

Well, Rudyard, he sure as hell was behind the ranges now. And *he* was the something that was lost.

He put a chunk of the fish into his mouth. No fish had ever tasted so good. He threw the other trout on the coals without bothering with the spit.

They ate in silence until both fish were finished, even the cheeks and tails and the skin. Afterward they leaned back against the walls, Paige with her eyes closed.

"Feel better?" he asked.

She nodded. "Much."

"Sorry I didn't have any almonds," he said, taking out his cigarettes. There were two left.

She opened her eyes. "Almonds?"

"Truite amandine," he said.

She smiled. "You *are* a cook, aren't you."

He opened the matchbook; four left.

"Have to be."

"Your wife—doesn't she cook?"

"I'm not—" he began. He lit the cigarette and blew out the smoke. "She died. Killed two years ago."

"Oh, David, I'm sorry. I should have known that. I've been so up to my neck in cost sheets that I haven't had time to learn about the people who made the magazine so great. I should have known about your wife. If we get back"—a look of guilt at this admission of fear flashed across her face and she amended it—"when we get back, I'd be grateful if you'd help me with the magazine and the people who work for it. I want you to be an important part of it."

He took a drag from the cigarette. "Don't worry. We'll get back."

"David—didn't you wonder why I came out here? I mean, the real reason."

"I figured you came for the waters."

"The waters?" she asked. "What waters?"

He tried to dismiss it lightly with a shrug and an attempt at a Claude Raines—Bogart imitation.

"What brought you to Casablanca? I came for the waters. There *are* no waters in Casablanca."

"Yes, I know. I saw the movie too. Ten times. Bogey takes a slow drag on his cigarette and answers, 'I was misinformed.' But, David, damn it,

I'm trying to be serious. I mean it—I need you.
Elliott's getting old and I need a strong man at the
top."

David didn't say anything.

After a while she said, "May I ask—were you
married long?"

He nodded. "Have a fourteen-year-old boy."

She was getting sleepy.

"Was it a good marriage?"

"My mother used to say whenever there were
more good times than bad times you had a good
marriage. Ours was good. At least from my side of
it."

"And she went on your assignments with you?"

He shook his head. "She was a homebody. And
we had the boy to take care of. Retarded. Great kid,
but—backward. She hated my going away—
thought it was too dangerous. Wanted me to be a—I
guess a commuter, PTA, country club, all that."

Suddenly Paige snapped awake at a frightening
noise outside.

"Lord, what was that?"

David smiled at her. "That, my dear, was the
most blood-curdling sound one can hear in the
forest—the great horned owl."

She lay back murmuring, "Haysoos, I thought it
was a mountain lion at the very least."

"A mountain lion wouldn't hurt you either,
unless it was hurt or cornered. Been very few attacks
on humans by mountain lions."

She was asleep. He threw some more branches on
the fire, then he picked up handfuls of leaves and
piled them around her. He put on his trousers, lay
down near her with a pile of leaves under his head
and barely remembered stretching out.

He woke up several hours later, cold and

dreaming that Walker, the gang leader, was in the cave. He threw a limb on the fire and the flames leaped up.

Paige stirred and opened her eyes. "Time to get up?" she murmured.

"No," he said. "Go to sleep."

"I was dreaming. About my horse. I was fifteen again and taking Comet over the jumps and my mother and father weren't divorced yet and they were watching me and applauding and all was right with the world. I was so happy then—that was the last year I was truly happy."

"Go back to your dream."

"God help the poor guy if I ever meet a man I love as much as Comet."

She closed her eyes. "What happened to her, David?"

"Who?" he said, knowing.

"You said she was killed."

He put another branch on the fire. "One day Elaine came in to the city from Connecticut to get a frame for a picture I loved. For my birthday. The shop was on 110th Street. She was on her way back toward the subway—broad daylight. Some teenage muggers slugged her, grabbed her purse. Her head hit the pavement. Never regained consciousness."

"Dear God!" Paige said.

"And she was the one who was always telling me to give up my career—that it was too dangerous."

"Oh Lord, I'm sorry, David."

"Go back to your dream, Paige. We've still got some sleeping time."

He put one more branch on the fire and lay back thinking of Elaine and their life of so many eons ago. And he thought about Paige's offer. Maybe it wouldn't be so bad. He wasn't getting any younger. But wasn't a desk job what he'd always been trying to avoid? Maybe part of the work would be in the field, though. It was all a long way away from here.

He awoke with the sun streaming into the cave and his feet very cold. He'd slept longer than he meant to. He shook Paige awake.

"Got to get going."

She stretched and got up, rubbing her upper arms and the shoulder that had been bruised in the car accident.

"How do you feel?" he asked as he pulled on his socks and boots.

"Fine." She nodded. "Pretty fine. Stiff as hell, actually."

She stood up. "I can't get your wife—her senseless death—out of my mind. It's like what my grandfather used to say: 'Life is a practical joke in the worst possible taste.'"

He picked up the camera case. "Let's go. Got to get across to that house."

But when they arrived at the river, now sparkling in the sun, he still had no idea how they were going to cross it.

The river was only thirty feet wide, but no one could wade across that torrent with its white rapids.

David walked upstream for a distance, but the river narrowed and the current was worse. Downstream a box canyon began, ruling out any attempt in that direction.

But there was a gnarled tree, one of whose limbs arched out over the river. The limb looked strong enough though its end was split as though by lightning. Not only was this their best chance, it was their only chance.

David tossed his aluminum case on top of a four-foot-high boulder that jutted out into the stream. Then he scrambled up behind it. He opened the case, took the nylon rope he had used to lower

himself from his aerie and snapped the lid closed.
He fashioned a noose at one end of the rope and
made a lasso. After swinging the loop around his
head twice he let it sail up toward the limb. The rope
hit the wood but fell back down into the water.
David retrieved it and tried again. This time the
rope slapped the wood and the noose curled around
the end. David drew it tight, then made a loop in the
end he was holding. He motioned to Paige and
reached down to haul her up to the rock.

"Foot!" he shouted over the roar of the river,
steadying her as she stood on one leg and put her
booted foot into the loop. She held on to the rope
with both hands. David pulled her back by the
waist, then shoved hard. She sailed out over the
water, her weight causing one foot to drag in the
riffles. When the arc took her over the other bank
she struggled to land but she couldn't get her foot
out of the noose. Back she swung over the water
toward David's outstretched arms. As she came
spinning into the rock, her free foot kicked out, hit
the aluminum case and knocked it into the water.

Steadying Paige, David watched with horror as
the case bobbed down the mountain in the foam of
the torrent. Oh God! he moaned. Oh God! He felt a
chunk of his life, all his work and training and
preparations were in that case, spinning out of sight.

"Oh, David!" Paige cried out.

David could feel a part of him drain out and die.
Not only the artistic loss, he felt the panic of the
financial burden return to his gut; there went the
payments on the house, the tuition on Chris' school.

"We can look for it, David! It's watertight, isn't
it?"

"Yes. Maybe it'll wash ashore. We'll look later."
But he knew he would never see those films

again. No article, no book, no money, no help for the condors.

Finally he said, "Let's get across this goddamned river."

Paige made it across on the next try, landing partially in the water but falling forward, grabbing a root and hauling herself up before the force of the water could yank her into the current. The rope dangled over the river, blown out almost flat by the wind that chased the water downstream. David slid down from the rock, found a thin branch and made a hook like a fire poker and climbed back up.

He retrieved the end of the rope by snagging it with the stick. Then he too swung across. Because rope was so valuable in the wilds, for nearly ten minutes he tried to save it but he couldn't work it off the branch. Finally he reached up the rope as far as he could and cut off a section, coiled it and put it in his pocket.

Then he led the way into the trees. There was a distinct trail here, as though it were a path frequently used to go to the water by deer.

In a moment they were in the shadow of the trees. David was trotting, and he urged Paige to keep up.

"Come on—we're near it."

Then he saw the flash through the branches directly in front of him.

"We're here!"

Cautiously, crouching, they stepped out into a clearing and saw in front of them a gigantic green tubular shape. David saw instantly what was catching the sunlight. It was a glass dome—the turret on top of a cracked airplane fuselage. The bomber lay with its nose down, tail fifteen feet in the air, leaves and vines and the dirt of decades camouflaging it. With its massive wings swept back it looked like some ancient bird, a pterodactyl, stuck in a tar pit.

"David—" Paige began questioningly, her disappointment making her voice tremble.

"B-17."

It was almost comical. Instead of a house and safety they find this—a fellow derelict. It had probably been here thirty years or more.

And if this had lain out here undetected for so long, what chance had they to be rescued?

He walked to the plane where the fuselage had cracked. He stepped into the dark hole and ducked as a bird—or was it a bat?—slapped past his face. The first thing he saw when his eyes grew accustomed to the gloom were parachute packs and rusted belts of machine gun bullets. Then he made out the leather-clad remains of a man lying on the floor. A shaft of sunlight coming down through the glass turret spotlighting his helmeted skull, made it into a ghastly imitation of Rembrandt's "Man in the Golden Helmet." Above the dead man was his weapon—twin .50's, dual mount, recoil operated, rusted into a brown mass. The air smelled foul and strands of cobwebs hung down like skeins of yarn. A weasel-like creature exploded out of the leaves and streaked past his legs.

David walked through the plane and saw two other figures slumped in the same position in which the accident had caught them. One had a pipe near the bones of his hand. A third was torn by some long-dead predator; a lizard skittered across the white rib cage.

In the cockpit the pilot and his copilot were slumped over the controls, the intercoms still around their bony throats, their tarnished officer's insignias on their shoulders.

It was eerie—like desecrating a mausoleum. He felt claustrophobic.

David walked back through the cabin, a knot of emotion in his throat as he reflected about the families of these men, who had never learned of the airmen's fate. He came to the tail section. The skeleton of a tail gunner was still in his cockpit. But strangely, his machine gun was not there, though its mount jetted empty in front of the grinning skull in the leather helmet. Who would have taken the weapon? Why?

He wanted to get out of there, but in the corner near him he saw a pile of sheep-lined coats—he and Paige could use something like that tonight if they were forced to spend another night in the wilds. And there were other bags of equipment—maybe steel thermos jugs, knives, tools still usable. Grisly as it seemed, this tragic event of so long ago might help them survive.

As he stepped forward, he heard a rattling sound. He jumped back and reached for the pistol in his pocket as he saw the mound of coats stir. The garments were writhing with dozens of small snakes. Their buzzing told him that they were young rattlers, each one as lethal as a full-grown snake.

David stumbled out of the plane. He walked fast to where Paige waited and took her by the wrist.

"What is it?" she asked.

"Let's get out of here."

He pushed her ahead of him down the trail leading away from the clearing. Suddenly he heard a snapping twig and thought he saw a man, almost a shadow, between the trees. But when he went toward it, his gun ready, he could see nothing. There was no one there—it was his nerves, he said to himself.

Nevertheless, for the next half an hour, as they went down the trail, he kept the pistol drawn and glanced back over his shoulder. He had the feeling that they were being watched and followed. Was it the men, the gang? If not, where were they—how far behind? He knew that they could never give up until they had the film in his pocket. He felt for it—yes, it was still there. At least he had that.

They came out of the trees as abruptly as they had entered. There were boulders still and the trail was steep. But way below was a greenness that promised gentle water that they had not yet encountered.

The sun scorched them as they slid down the mountain, and it was as though they had never had any water back at the river. He found himself thinking of the plane. Why would someone take the machine gun—and why would the thief not then report the relic to the authorities? But it was hard to think now of anything but fatigue and thirst. Paige was stumbling more often now.

"Got to—got to drink," Paige gasped.

"Keep going," David panted. "Soon."

He had seen the Fremont cottonwoods. And in another hour they would hear the river.

Chapter Five

"Water!" he shouted.

He took her by the hand and began running toward the sound. Moving across the grassy meadow was ridiculously easy and they ran with a drunken giddiness into the shade of the cotton-woods, dappled about by gold dollars of sunlight, running toward the roar of the waterfall. Grass and sod became gravel and sand. They kept running across the wet rocks and into one of the pools that formed below the fifteen-foot fall.

They tumbled forward and lay in the shock of the water, dunking their heads, drinking and spitting.

When David stood up, his clothing slimed to his body, heavy and binding. He sloshed his way to the bank and stripped off the jacket. His trousers clung to his legs like wet wallpaper, and he had to struggle to get them off. His shoelaces snarled, the socks knotted on themselves. At last he fought himself free of it all and, naked except for his shorts, turned to stride back into the pool. Paige's clothes already lay neatly stacked on a boulder jutting from the opposite shore. She was lying in her bra and panties, with her face completely under water; he could see she was drinking. He waded rapidly to her and pulled her head up by her hair.

"Not all at once."

"It's so good," she gasped. "Never tasted anything so good."

"Too much'll make you sick."

He looked back up to the mountain they had come down. No sign of the enemy, no sound. What was the John Wayne thing?—"The Indians are quiet tonight." "Yeah, too quiet...." They had to be up there somewhere.

A breeze whipped across the pool, sending ripples along the water. Several leaves spiraled from the trees and floated near the shore. He felt a sudden chill and realized it would soon be night and it was going to be cold again. And did they dare make a fire? No—no fire out here in the open; this was not like the cave.

And he was hungry again and weak. He glanced across at Paige. She was floating full length now, her shoulders and buttocks resting on the rounded stones in the water. She'd be ravenous too. There should be more trout in these pools. They could eat them raw. And there was probably watercress or something similar. Escape from the pursuing gang was the primary worry, but the immediate goal was shelter for tonight. He studied the stand of trees. He would make a lean-to with a couple of "Y" forked branches stuck into the ground and a branch across on which he would lean bushy branches. Paige needed rest—she couldn't go on much farther; she looked half asleep in the water.

Suddenly he heard a noise behind him. He whirled, and between the boles of the trees he found himself looking into a pair of penetratingly yellow eyes. They were glaring out from a hollow in the brambles across the pool from him.

He eased back toward the shore where he'd left his jacket with the pistol. He pushed his almost naked body across the bank, never losing sight of the rabid eyes.

He eased closer to his jacket.

"I wouldn't touch that, mister." The voice came from the clump of brambles. "Not if I was you, that is."

David hesitated. Then he whirled, flopped out onto the bank, dived onto the jacket and, rolling over on the sand, came to his elbows with the pistol aimed at the hollow. The eyes had disappeared, but there was a growl—more the snarl of a mountain cat not twenty feet to his left. David twisted toward the sound. He could see nothing but tree trunks and underbrush. He looked back at the bramble bushes; there was nothing there—just the bushes and the trees and beyond a grassy slope and the sky.

"I told you, mister, you hadn't ought to touch that gun."

This time the voice came from behind David's left shoulder.

He swiveled on his knees, gun jabbed out. It pointed at a stand of shrubs. There was no man.

Then he heard the ominous double-click and the heavy machined slap of a well-oiled carbine being cocked. The sound came from above and behind his neck. The muzzle of the gun was pushed between his shoulder blades.

"Now I want you to drop it."

David did, glancing across to Paige. She was sitting up in the water, covering her nakedness with her arms and knees.

"Up," commanded the voice.

David stood up.

"Turn around."

And he saw that it was a stick that had been shoved into his back. The man held the carbine in his right hand like a pistol and a foot-long stick in his left.

The man snorted. "Old trick but a good un." He threw away the stick and took the rifle in both hands. "That way your man can't do no fancy spinnin' and knockin'."

David stared at his captor with amazement. He was short—not over five feet tall; barefooted, he was dressed in a pair of almost white jeans and a tattered but clean T-shirt. Below the yellow-white hair, the face with its sunken eyes was of an indeterminate age—either that of a ravaged young man who had lived through the sewers of hell or that of a well-preserved old man who maintained the vitality of someone half his age. His cheeks were so sunken he seemed to be eating on them. Above the pale eyes were eyebrows so heavy they could have been cut from mattress stuffing and pasted on as an afterthought. And David knew instinctively that this wood gnome was not a part of the motorcycle gang. But was he friend or enemy?

"Speak up, mister! Who are you?"

David cleared his voice.

"No lies now!" The little man brandished his rifle almost comically and drew back his lips in a snarl, revealing more gum than teeth.

David sighed. "Mister, we've been through a lot. She—Miss Evans—has about had it."

The man glanced across at Paige, then he looked away as though embarrassed by her nakedness.

"Well, that don't concern me none. What you doin' out here in nowhere land is what I need to know."

David sucked in a long breath, "There was a gang—a killing. Do you know if there is a ranger station around here?"

The man didn't seem to understand.

"A house?" David simplified.

The man thought for a moment, then nodded.

David's hopes rose. "Near here someplace?"

"Might say so," the little man conceded grudgingly. Then he snapped. "A killing, you say?"

David shivered and pointed to his heap of clothing. "Mister, I'll tell you everything. But a man can't talk naked and you waving that cannon all over hell."

A grin whipped across their captor's face at language he understood. He nodded and cradled his gun. David started to put on his wet clothes and motioned for Paige to do the same. The little man lowered his eyes when she stood up and kept his gaze on the ground until she was dressed.

Then, wordlessly, he picked up the pistol, stuffed it in his waistband, motioned them to follow and set off into the bushes. David and Paige trailed behind on a path that ran parallel to the stream. The man ahead hunched in a crouch and trotted with a gait more foxlike than human. David and Paige were forced to crouch down under the branches that joined above the tunnels formed by the undergrowth. Clearly this was a trail used only by animals and the strange creature guiding them.

David hung back for a second, turned and

whispered to Paige, "He's taking us to the ranger station."

But even as he said the words, he knew it was too good to be the truth.

Chapter Six

Their clothing had almost dried in the afternoon heat when they came to the last of the tunnel-like growth and stepped into a great meadow.

Blue-green grass bent in waves in an almost perfect circle for a mile about them; it was surrounded by the rise of granite cliffs. The lower end of the meadow was swampy where the stream split into fingers; the upper end was cultivated. David could see corn stalks and the plowed rows of a truck garden. A lone cow cropped grass near a brown mule.

In the middle of the meadow stood a ramshackle barn, gray-white with age, the color of their captor's faded jeans—innocent of paint for decades. Except for an outhouse behind the barn and some fencing there was nothing else to be seen. There was no sign of a road in or out of the valley.

"That the place you been lookin' for, mister?" The little man jabbed his rifle toward the barn. Now it seemed to David that he had a cockney lilt to his speech, or perhaps a hint of a Scottish burr.

David sucked in his breath. "I think you're making a joke with us. This is not the house we were looking for."

The little man laughed. "Fine house to me. No joke. To me and Maddy it's the best house in the world."

Paige, looking faint, drew herself up straight and, with a boardingschool huskiness, said to the man, "May I sit down, sir?"

Their captor stared at her without answering. David held out his hand. "Sit down, Paige."

She took his hand and sagged to her knees and onto her haunches.

"Tuckered, ain't she?"

"She's been through—a hell of a lot."

Abruptly the little man hunkered to his knees. "Rest a mite."

David hesitated a moment before easing himself down near Paige. After a minute he said, "Sir, we'd be much obliged—"

"Name ain't sir! Left them bastards in the Navy. Name's Starky."

The rooster was trying to be friendly. David stretched out his hand. "My name's Brand—David Brand."

"Can't remember fancy names. I'll call you Brandy."

They shook hands solemnly.

"Starky, the house—ranger station—must be around here—someplace?"

Starky shook his head. "Nowhere near."

David glanced around at the cliffs and the woods behind them. The little man was right—there was nothing anywhere in view but this barnlike structure, and out there somewhere was a group of men bent on killing them.

"I wonder," David began hesitantly, for he had no assurance that this man was friendly, "have you seen any men today—a group—"

Starky's eyes hopped from one face to the other. "Don't get many callers here 'bouts. Not people callers—mostly critters."

"I heard that one back there at the pool, the mountain lion."

The man stared at him blankly for an instant, then his face darkened and he snapped, "Hell, that weren't no mountain lion! That was a bobcat! Can't you tell a bobcat when you hear one?"

And the next instant the air was cut with that screaming snarl. It came from the edge of the woods behind them. David jerked about. The scream stopped as abruptly as it had begun. He snapped back to look at Starky; the little man's head was thrown back, his mouth open as he laughed soundlessly at the sky. He was slapping his right hand against his knee in glee.

"Gotcha!" Starky coughed. "Gotcha twice!"

David realized that they were this little man's captives and if they were to survive he had to be humored.

"That was you? That was really you?"

The man held the tip of his finger up to his lips, signaling silence, and pointed to a spot farther away. And again the cat scream split the silence, but this time it was, as the man indicated, from farther down the meadow. And except for the bulge of the

veins in the scrawny neck, the sucking-in of his
cheeks and thinness of his lips, David would have
had no hint that Starky was responsible for the
sounds.

"That's my talent." The little man grinned.
"Comes natural to me. But you can learn it—take
mebbe a meadowlark. Simple, that one is. First off
you hit a straight whistle—" His lips didn't pucker,
but a tiny hole appeared between them and a sharp,
clean whistle sounded.

"Next you say the words *heed-dah-lah* as you
whistle."

The call of a meadowlark rippled out across the
afternoon. A second later, there was the answering
cry from a bird down the field. It was fascinating,
but David couldn't help searching the hills. "You're
sure you haven't seen—"

"Who's to know?" Starky stood up abruptly.
"Let's get this woman to where Maddy can care for
her. And Brandy, you got a smart cut there
Maddy'll fix for you, too. She's got healin' hands,
Maddy does."

The three of them walked toward the barn.
Halfway there, Starky slid from the path like a
shadow. Ten feet away, he parted the grass, reached
down and pulled up a rusted steel trap. A dead
rabbit dangled from the sawtooth jaws.

Starky released the trap, removed the rabbit and
reset the trap. Carrying the carcass by its hind legs,
he returned to the path saying, "Don't like traps.
But bullets cost money and Blinky's got to eat.
Blinky won't eat nothing once it's alive."

He walked along beside them, the rifle cradled in
his left arm, the rabbit swinging by his right side.
"Tell you who gets the rabbits 'round here that
oughta by rights go to Blinky. Ole Rusty gets 'em,
that's who."

A few steps along the path, Starky slowed and signaled them to stop. He tucked both the rifle and carcass to him with his left arm, raised both hands to his mouth and blew a quavering series of whines— similar to sounds David had made as a boy by blowing against a blade of grass between his thumbs.

Immediately a fox appeared on the path ahead of him. Head up, ears alert, it trotted toward them in quick bounds, stopped warily, studied them, then turned and loped easily away into the grass, his luxurious tail undulating gracefully behind him. For a moment, David had felt certain it was going to trot up to Starky like a family pet.

Starky chuckled. "Strange folk scare him off. He comes when I call like a wounded rabbit. Used to fool him when he was a pup that way. Won't eat nothing dead—different from Blinky. Takes all kinds." The little man suddenly sobered. "I oughta kill ole Rusty so's there'd be plenty of dead rabbits for Blinky, or I oughta kill Blinky so's there'd be rabbits for Rusty. Can't figure it out rightly."

As they neared the ancient barn shaded by cottonwoods, David saw the building was no longer so much a working farm building as a patchwork homestead. Two large windows had been installed in the wood on either side of the conventional front door. Other windows had been set into the front of the building in a seemingly random pattern. Boards of all sizes and various degrees of aging testified to many years of repair; a portion of the swaybacked roof had been recently recovered with new handcut wood shakes.

Flower boxes red with geraniums were set beneath the lower windows, and a surprisingly sophisticated patio had been built in the yard. Then slices of wood were set down in a bed of river stones to form the terrace. Halved tree trunks joined to make a hexagon of benches around a five-foot-wide stump that served as a table. A turkey moved in the bushes at the far side of the patio, and David heard chickens clucking somewhere.

Starky shouted, "Maddy! Maddy, we need you!"

As they crossed the patio the door opened and a young woman wiping her hands on a dish towel stepped out into the afternoon sun. Hair the color of maple syrup streaked with honey hung below her shoulders; she wore the same white man's T-shirt and faded jeans as Starky but her feet were shod in hand-made moccasins.

Her skin appeared almost the color of her hair; her breasts thrust upward, and the pink of her nipples was apparent through the shirt, which swung loose over her narrow waist and the tops of the jeans that clung to her hips.

Her eyes seemed to catch David's and hold him hypnotized: they were a color he had never seen before, an incredible violet—half-lidded and un-blinking.

She moved toward them with the flat-footed grace of a Calypso dancer, her arms slightly out from her sides, hands tilted up at the wrists with her palms toward the ground. And she seemed to move to a secret music—setting each foot in its proper place at the proper time to accompany the sway of her hips.

Softly she asked, "Who are they, Pa?"

"They'll tell us when they're ready." He set the rifle and the rabbit on one of the logs. "They come by Chimney Ridge and they're real done in." Gently he touched Paige's shoulder and brought her to his daughter. "See to her, Maddy, she is beat bad and hungry. Brandy there's got a bad hand, too."

The tawny woman put her arm about Paige and
guided her into the house.

Starky cocked his head and studied David
alertly. "Brandy, you sit, and I'll bring you some
medicinal." He chuckled and turned to the house.

Halfway to the door, Starky stopped, laughed
delightedly, turned and pointed a bony finger
toward David. "Brandy's your name and brandy's
my tipple."

Minutes passed, then Starky appeared behind
David with a jug in one hand and David's pistol in
the other. It was incredible the way the man could
move around noiselessly.

"Had to make sure." He shook his head. "Some
say Starky's simple. Mebbe so, mebbe not. But not
so simple he leaves no man at his back with a chance
at a gun without first making sure."

David looked up at him, puzzled.

Starky thrust the pistol at him. "Take your gun
back, Brandy. Starky don't hold with guns mostly
anyways."

David opened his hand and Starky laid the pistol
in it.

"Now you take a swig, Brandy, it's a real face-
tightener."

David put the pistol in his pocket and accepted
the jug from the man. It was chilled and beaded with
drops of water. He lifted it cautiously to his lips and
tipped it little by little until the first liquid slid over
his tongue. When he had a moderate mouthful, he
swallowed.

The brandy slid smoothly down his throat and
into his stomach. He sighed with satisfaction.

Starky took the jug from him, watching for
approval. He prompted, "Mighty fine, ain't it?
Don't that tighten the face?"

Then the alcohol began to become warm in his throat and stomach; speedily it became hot and then so hot it flamed. David opened his mouth wide and exhaled hard.

Starky beamed. "Mighty medicinal. Mighty fine."

David nodded as he sucked his breath back in over the burning throat; the liquid dynamite now seemed to lie on his empty stomach, glowing like a ship's boilerplate. He whispered, "Mighty fine." The menace of the killer gang seemed to recede, but he asked again: "A group of men—you sure you didn't—"

"Who's to know?" Starky said enigmatically.

Starky hoisted the jug up on his elbow, craned his head sideways and poured the liquid into his mouth. He poured and continued pouring, his Adam's apple working, sliding up and down as he swallowed. He continued until David wondered if he wasn't about to drown. Finally the old man lowered the jug and gasped joyously, "Mighty medicinal!"

And now that the fire in his guts had died down, David realized the little man was indeed right. He felt one hell of a lot better. He accepted the jug back when Starky passed it to him and took another swallow, and nodded appreciatively at Starky. The alcohol continued to work its magic; he began to feel lightheaded, but not so hungry, and his fatigue and soreness were dropping away from him.

"Starky, we got to get out of here early in the morning. Before the gang comes. We should be traveling now, but it's too dark and we don't know the way. Will you show us the way tomorrow?"

"Who's to know?" said Starky guardedly. "That gang—is it connected with the airplane?"

"The airplane?"

"The one that crashed."

This man was crazier than David had thought. "No, Starky, the gang has no connection with the airplane." No point in telling him that no one had been alive around that plane for over thirty years.

"Well, who's to know?" Starky said slyly.

"If you don't use the gun," David asked, "how do you kill? The deer and things you and Maddy eat."

"Wait in the woods, near the trails, near the water. Sometimes I call 'em in to me. Move very quiet and then it's all over. Quick." Starky held up his left hand as though pulling back a deer's head, and his right flashed horizontally in front of him.

He was holding a bowie knife with a six-inch blade that had been honed to a narrow sliver of steel. David hadn't seen him draw it; there seemed no possible place it could have been concealed by his meager clothing.

"Quick," he repeated. "Starky doesn't like to hurt anybody."

He chortled happily again. "There's more! And plenty more." He put the knife back into a sheath sewn in the blue jeans just above the knee. He picked up the jug and swung it across to David. As he was sipping, the little man added, "I'm late with Blinky's supper."

He put his thumb and forefinger to his Adam's apple and made a hissing deep in his throat. Instantly there was a thrashing sound in the shrubs at the end of the patio and the bird David had taken to be a turkey hopped out of the bushes, answering with the same sound Starky had made.

It resembled a birth-deformed bald eagle with naked head and neck; one mammoth wing extended in excitement, the other lay flat against its body.

Starky reached down, picked up the dead rabbit and flung it to the bird.

As the bird hopped awkwardly toward the rabbit, David gasped, "My God, you've got a condor—a pet condor!"

Starky nodded. "That's what they call him. I call him Blinky. Call him Blinky," he cackled, " 'cause he never blinks."

David studied the bird. One of its wings was splintered and bandaged and there was a chain tether fastened to one of its legs. Its head was bright orange as was the beak that probed into the entrails of the rabbit it held pinned under one claw. It was somehow obscene to see a member of this rarefied species captive, though of course it was for its own survival.

Starky sat back down and lifted the jug. "Poor dumb sumbitches," he said. "No power in their beaks. Rabbit's about all they can handle. When it comes to something with a tough hide like a cow or horse, they got to get at the meat through them natural openings. Seen a deer carcass the other day one of them birds had turned inside out—like peeling a glove off your hand."

David shook his head in disbelief at what he was watching. This man must certainly be the only person in the world who could talk the language of the condors.

"Starky, do you know that's one of the rarest birds in all the world?"

Starky scoffed. "They's a whole bunch of 'em right up here."

"Less than fifty. And that's it. That's all there are in the whole world. Do you have any idea what a bird like that's worth—say to a zoo or a scientific research institute?"

Starky stuck the tip of his finger into his ear and scratched meditatively; David's excitement had obviously brought a new idea home to him. "Worth money, is he? Blinky's worth money?" He grinned at David foxily. "Maybe a hundred dollars?"

David scowled in amazement.

The little man shifted uncomfortably. "I need a hundred dollars for the doctor."

"My God, Starky, that bird's worth more than a hundred dollars. Much, much more."

Starky's lupine smile returned. He whispered, "Two hundred, mebbe?"

David shrugged hopelessly; their worlds were too far apart.

Starky gazed across the patio at the bird eating. "Not a pretty one, is he? Mighty ugly to watch him feed—specially on a week-old carcass. But I reckon that's the way thing's supposed to be."

"How'd you get him?"

"Eight, ten mile back. Been shot—hunters must of shot him." Then he shook his head vigorously. "No! No! I ain't going to sell Blinky. Not for two hundred dollars, even. Not to no zoo. Blinky belongs up here—belongs up here like me. And when his wing's well, he's going to fly 'way. Then he's going to have to find his own food and he's going to remember ol' Starky."

When the monstrous bird had gulped the last hunk of the rabbit, it raised its rump in contentment and ejected a stream of cream-colored excrement. Then it hopped to the wooden washtub at the edge of the patio and preened its black feathers.

Starky took another swig from the jug as he watched. "Funny critter. Eats only dead meat but can't stand the stink of death on himself."

It spite of his fatigue David felt a sudden

excitement. It was only a wild possibility, but if it would work it would surely be the simplest way to preserve the species—to try to breed the bird under control. As far as he knew there was only one other condor in captivity—a female in the Los Angeles Zoo. If he could convince Starky to assist in breeding them—to at least let them borrow Blinky!

The other idea that had come to him was that one of the reasons the condors in the wild were not breeding as they should was lack of food; there simply wasn't the amount of carrion that there used to be. So—why not implement a regular food lift to them? Animals put away in the pounds of California, animal carcasses killed on the highways, slaughterhouse discards? Assured of regular food, the big birds might start breeding at a better rate.

As the ideas were spinning in his head, Maddy came out of the door carrying a tray with a cracked porcelain washbowl filled with water, bandages and iodine on it. She moved across the patio so smoothly that the water appeared mirror-smooth in the bowl. She smiled. "She's resting just fine."

David stood up. "Thank you very much, Maddy." And he couldn't help thinking it was an ugly name for such a beautiful woman.

She walked to him, set the tray on the table section, and sat on the tree stump next to his. He sat again and let his eyes drift down across her.

Her voice was low and soothing when she said, "Now let me care for that hand. Pa says it's hurt."

David lifted his left hand. The cut no longer bled, but it was ugly and stiff. She laid her hand fleetingly on his right arm, slid it along his forearm, across his knuckles, and lightly raised it, turned it and held it between her own. Gently she bent each of the fingers forward in turn.

"Hurt?" she asked.

David continued to hold his other hand in front of her, the wounded palm toward her face. Again she bent the fingers of the wrong hand, now moving her thumb deeper toward the knuckles.

"Does it hurt when I do this?"

"No," David whispered. "No, that doesn't hurt." And he knew then that the violet eyes were blind.

Chapter Seven

"Light and dark, that's all she can see," Starky said, nodding, after Maddy had finished tending to David's hand and returned to the house. "Started happening some time back."

"Have you taken her to a specialist?" David asked, immediately thinking of John Barkin, his neighbor in Connecticut who was considered by many to be the foremost ophthalmologist in the country.

"They's only one doc in Piru. Says it ain't going to get no better, probably. But we could take her off to some famous place if we had the money. Still, he says they probably can't do no more than he can."

Suddenly, without getting up, his feet did a little jig and he passed David the jug. "Brandy's your name," he sang. "M'tipple's the same..."

Maddy opened the door. "Dinner's ready—such as it is."

"Such as it is!" mocked Starky, getting up unsteadily. "Bes' cook in the world, Maddy is. You married, son?"

"No," said David.

David got up and they went into the house, Starky holding the door and ushering David with a bow. David took one last look around in the dusk— not a sign of the men. Could they have given up the chase? Or were they lying in wait for them to come out of this valley in the morning?

The livingroom-kitchen combination was larger than David had imagined. A fire glowed in the huge fireplace made of colored boulders. There were skins on the floor and chairs made of antlers. An old-fashioned wood stove dominated the center of the kitchen.

The room was set three steps down from the front door. As soon as he had descended, David understood why. The kitchen "sink" was formed of stone, and a stream of spring water flowed from the wooden trough outside and passed over a rock slab into the bowl. The overflow spilled into another wooden trench, ran down the length of the room and disappeared into the far wall. There were skins on the floor and some were hung as partitions for other rooms off the kitchen.

"Care to wash up, Brandy?" Starky said, pointing to a doorway. "Take a leak?"

David nodded, and pushing aside the deerskin he stepped into the room. He could see now that the water that was conducted from the kitchen sink traveled through the hole in the wall to the bathroom sink, then dropped into an oil drum which had been cut in half lengthwise. Raised on stones, it had a kerosene heater under it. The water that flowed out of the bottom of the bathtub was directed along a trench under a wooden commode in the corner. David smiled at Starky's ingenuity.

When David came out, Maddy had the venison stew on the table and kerosene lamps lit. As they ate, David told them of the ordeal he and Paige had been through, trying to sort it all out in his own mind as he went along.

Starky would mutter from time to time, "Dirty buggers!"

When David finished, Starky stood up, pounding his fist into his palm. "They's some connection! Gotta be. And there's something mighty frisky goin' on!"

"What do you mean?"

"Tell him about the plane," Maddy said. "The plane that crashed."

David nodded knowingly. "I saw it up on the mountain there. Old B-17—"

"No—no—no!" Starky shouted each word separately as though dealing with a torpid child. "Not *that* wreck! The new one!"

Now David felt confused. "They make a habit of crashing in here? I've only seen one plane fly over in the last three weeks."

Starky held up two fingers. Then he said, "Two! Two planes crashed. One crashes 'bout thirty years ago and Starky sees it happen. All dead. Then three days ago another plane comes over, sounding sick. Little silver plane. I don't see it crash, but it sure exploded bad. Figure they ought to hear it all the way to Piru." He gestured toward the mountains. "Over there. More than an hour away, way down the ravine an' all broke up. The smoke was something fierce and it smelt worse. Mebbe worst smell I ever recollect—'ceptin' when the barns went up at the racetrack where I was the exercise boy."

"Did you search the plane?" David asked.

"No," said Starky. "Left everything zactly like I found it. Same's I did thirty years ago with that big one."

He squirmed uncomfortably. "Don't want to get mixed up with nothing like that. Don't want 'thorities, government people, comin' 'round askin' questions." He sprang up. "Well, so maybe I did take a little peek. But just one—after the fire cooled off. Nothing in there 'cept antlers an' bones an' burnt carcasses. Nothing of no value to nobody."

David thought for a moment. "Sort of an expensive way to poach game."

"Well," said Starky, dismissing the subject, "who's to know?"

He tilted the jug but it was empty. He glanced at Maddy, who was doing the dishes, and whispered behind his hand to David, "Don't fret."

He took the kerosene lamp and motioned for David to follow him. He led the way toward the back of the house. On the big wall of the building which had once been a barn, David saw a remarkable thing. Covering the entire area was a primitive mural. David recognized it as an accurate representation of this meadow where they were now—the barn, the cow, the mule, Maddy and Starky posing stiffly in the patio. There were all types of birds and animals—Rusty the fox, some condors, plus bears and cougars.

"Starky—did you do that?"

"Maddy—she did it. Couple of years ago, before her eyes went. She always was a good drawer. She got this idea from the Chumash caves up yonder."

"The what?"

"Chumash Indians used to live all around here. Painted pictures in their caves."

But Starky was prouder of his springhouse out in

back, a sunken shack with screen windows. Here in its coolness hung smoked sides of meat and ribbons of jerky. Tins of milk floated in the icy spring water, tubs of butter—and dozens of jugs of homemade "medicinal." Starky handed the lamp to David and extracted a dripping jug, working his lips in anticipation.

They went back into the house and on the way to the kitchen Starky pushed back a deerskin curtain and held the light up so that David could see Paige.

"Doin' fine," said Starky, belching.

She was lying on the bed, her face scrubbed clean, her hair brushed, and a calm expression on her sleeping features. She looked about sixteen years old and very pretty, not at all the tough New York career woman she aspired to be.

"She your girl?" asked Starky.

"No," said David.

In the kitchen David said, "Thank you—very much. For taking care of her."

Maddy dismissed it with a smile and a gesture with her hand. As she finished doing the dishes, David sagged to a chair. His head began to nod and his eyelids felt as though they had coins taped to them.

"How did you get here?" he asked. "What brought you here?"

"Nothin' to tell," said Starky. "Was in the Navy. Machinist's mate. Did somethin' they didn't like. Cleared out there."

David looked questioningly at him.

"I cleared out—AWOL—'fore they could lock me up! Guess they're still lookin' for me. But if they try to take me, they'll sure as hell know they're in a fight!"

Maddy filled in with some more information: Starky found out that his wife had divorced him and run off with their infant daughter. All through the war he'd vowed to "get away from all the goddamn people, go someplace where there weren't none of them buggers bent on destroying each other and the world." With the little money he managed to save, he'd bought this piece of land, considered almost worthless because of its remoteness. But he'd kept in touch with Maddy and then three years ago she had joined him.

"It was after that bastard of a husband of hers had—"

"Getting late, Pa!" Maddy took off her apron. She hesitated in front of David. "I'll look in on Paige during the night. And—I'll see you in the morning."

"Good night," Starky said.

She walked out of the kitchen and through the deerskin strips to her bedroom. Starky lurched to his feet and held out the jug to David.

"Tipple's m'name," he slurred, "an' Brandy's m'game."

Suddenly, incredibly, David heard music. He recognized it as something from an opera, "Médita- tion" from *Thaïs*, and it sounded far away and long ago—and up here in this wild place, surreal.

Starky saw his startled look. "That's just Maddy's Victrola. She traded one of her—whatcha call 'ems—things she weaves—for it in Sisquoc. Here, you need a little."

David shook his head. "Tomorrow's going to be rough. I'm going to get some sleep."

Starky nodded. He pointed to the room where Maddy had gone. "Good night."

"But that's your daughter's room," David said.

He nodded. "And you'll oblige Starky by laying with her."

David smiled. "If it's the same to you, I'll just stretch out in front of the fireplace."

"Listen, Brandy. Starky's been pretty good to you and your friend, right?" He fumbled the jug to his mouth, took a drink and then cradled it in his arms. "Now you're going to do Starky a favor. You lay with my daughter. What chance has she got out here? Blind, out here in no-man's land. Normal girl needs laying with. And Starky—how about poor old Starky, eh? Who cares what he needs? What does he need? I'll tell you what—a grandson—a grandson to help him work the fields and enjoy the streams and the hills. So you get in there and oblige my daughter and oblige Starky. And do it damn quick!"

Any ideas of laughing this off as a joke faded when David looked at the little man's eyes, crossed in their fury like a wolverine's. He was afraid that Maddy could hear their conversation.

"I tell you what," said David. He yawned and got up slowly. "Your daughter is mighty attractive, beautiful, and tomorrow we can talk about—"

In spite of the liquor he had consumed, Starky was on his feet in an instant, a knife flashing in his right hand while his left clutched David's shirtfront.

"You'll oblige Starky," he snarled, "or he'll have to treat you like one of the deer he kills with no more thought than he would a piss-ant!"

David leaned back away from the blade. He swallowed and nodded. When Starky slowly let go, David turned and walked to the room. He looked back at Starky briefly and saw the man, smiling and waving him on with his knife. David pushed the deerskin aside and went in.

It was a large room with animal hides on the floor and a loom in the middle. Maddy was just getting into the four-poster. By the light of the kerosene lamp on the table he could see the long hair hanging loose, the lithe body under the white nightgown. A wind-up phonograph was in a corner playing a syrupy version of the romantic *Thaïs* by a symphony orchestra, all of whose members would have to be dead.

"I'm sorry—" he began.

"Brandy?"

"My real name is David," he said uncomfortably. "David Brand. And I'm sorry about this. Your father—"

"That's all right," she said. "Come in."

"The truth is—he seems a little—maybe violent. I'll just wait here till he goes to sleep."

"You might have to wait a long time for Pa to pass out. I'm sorry he forced you to come in here."

"You heard?"

She didn't say anything as she adjusted the bedclothes.

The record came to an end. "Would you put it on again?"

He turned the handle on the phonograph and put the needle back at the beginning. "My mother used to play that in the evening after teaching school," he said. "On a rented piano—in Big Timber, Montana."

"It's my favorite," she said. "It came with the Victrola. That and a Brahms concerto and two Vincent Lopez foxtrots and three dozen cactus needles."

Her skin was the color of a mountain lion's against the white sheets. But it was her eyes that fascinated him. They did not look blind and they were beautiful with a color that seemed constantly to vary. Now they were the blue of the sky in a Vermeer painting.

"If I ever get out of this mess," he said, "I'll get you some records—a lot of records."

"The lamp," she said. "Turn it out if you want. I—I guess it's still a habit to turn off a light when it's time to go to bed."

"I'll see if your father's asleep."

Maddy smiled. "Am I so ugly, then?"

"No, no," he murmured.

He stepped forward and sat on the bed.

She reached out and ran her fingers over his features.

"A good face," she said. She turned back the covers. "You must be exhausted."

"I don't like the name Maddy," he said. "I'll call you Madelaine."

"Come to bed."

He stepped out of his clothes and left them where they fell. She moved over for him as he got into bed in his shorts. A peace came over him, and his last thought before he fell asleep was that the phonograph was still on and how beautiful *Thaïs* sounded, even on a wind-up Victrola with cactus needles.

He did not wake up again until early the next morning, when he felt a hand clutching him by the shoulder and shaking him.

Chapter Eight

"Brandy!" Starky's voice was hoarse with urgency, and David smelled his stale breath as he opened his eyes. "They're comin'!"

David threw back the covers, glancing at Maddy, who was sitting up in bed. The room was barely light in the gray dawn.

"Hurry, Mad!" rasped Starky. "You got to get the woman up! We gotta hide you all!"

David pulled on his clothes as Starky talked. "Airplane, circling, looking how to land!"

David could hear the plane now. He stuffed his shirt in and put on his coat, feeling the pistol in one pocket and the piece of rope in the other. Starky tugged at his arm. They went into the kitchen and looked out the window.

"There she be!"

David saw a yellow single-engine plane. Flying very low around the bowl of the valley, its left wing tipped almost vertically so that the pilot could check the terrain for landing. Where had they obtained a plane? and so soon?

"Smoothest field's on the other side of the house," said Starky. "Soon's he gets past this side, we go out."

The plane was so close that David could make out its number. Paige and Maddy came into the kitchen, Paige still squirming into her boots. Her hair was tangled and her face was puffy with sleep, but he could see that her eyes were clear and that she had recouped her strength.

She looked up as the plane seemed to compress as it swung to straight-on, still tipped to its side. David saw her chapped lips part and then close firmly. The gesture was determined. For the first time he felt he had an ally rather than a liability.

"So soon," she said with a shudder.

"Probably holds three or four men," David said.

Starky suddenly commanded, "Now!"

He went out the kitchen door, snatching his carbine off the gun rack as he did. They followed him around the corner. He stopped at the woodbin which ran along the side of the house. Starky put down his rifle, lifted the lid of the bin, and propped it up with a stick. The box was a quarter filled with three-foot logs piled lengthwise. Starky reached in and began throwing out the logs, two at a time. David imitated him, and when Paige saw what they were doing, she helped.

"Could put you in the springhouse under the planks," Starky panted, "or in the haystack. But think this is better."

When most of the logs were out Starky said: "Ma'am, you get in this end."

Starky and David helped Maddy in next to Paige
and they lay huddled together on the bottom of the
bin. Starky took a log and jammed it down
crosswise against the two sides of the bin until it was
only a few inches over the women's legs. He took
two more logs and jammed them down at two-foot
intervals, and David pushed one down over their
heads. Then, across these, Starky and David laid
some other logs lengthwise. When the women were
completely covered, Starky handed David the rifle.

"Only two bullets in it, but it's better than
nothin'." He pointed to the remaining space. "Get
in."

"But what about you?" asked David.

"Better I be out there or they'll think we're all
hidin'."

"They'll think you helped us get away!"

"Starky'll take care of Starky."

David felt in his coat pocket and pulled out the
length of rope.

"Here—use this."

Starky looked at it uncomprehending, then he
smiled.

"Good thinkin', Brandy."

David swung up into the bin and curled into a
fetal position, his feet just past the women's heads,
the rifle barrel clutched to his chest. Starky jammed
a log crosswise above David's body and then piled
the remaining wood on top. He pulled the stick
away and the lid banged down.

"You all right?" David whispered.

"Yes," whispered Paige and Maddy together.

He could make out their forms in the light that
filtered through the cracks in the bin. There was a
knothole at David's end, and by twisting his head he
could see Starky, who was running to the house,
stooping to pick up a shingle as he did. He went to

the apricot tree near the patio. Starky's back was to David, but he could see the man fumbling with the front of his clothes for a moment. Then David saw him reach up and loop the rope around a branch and make it tight. The other end he tied to his right wrist.

David couldn't see the plane—it was still on the other side of the house. But he could hear the pilot clearing the engine's throat; then the silence as the plane touched down and the motor being cut back in as the pilot taxied across the field. The plane came into David's view and he watched as it came up within two hundred feet of the house and then passed just outside of his field of vision and he heard the engine cough and die.

In a matter of minutes, three men came into David's sight. They were of average height, nondescript. One was fat, but it was not Walker; all were dressed like the rest of the motorcycle gang except the pilot, who seemed more stylish. He was the only new one—the others David remembered from his first sight of the gang. All had pistols drawn as they advanced toward the house.

David felt his heart jabbing, as though banging against his rib cage. Only three of them! He had two bullets in Starky's rifle, and the pistol in his pocket contained one bullet. Conceivably, he could stick the rifle barrel through the knothole and pick off two of them. But then what?

The problem was solved for him when into view strode a fourth man. Very tall, thin, round-shouldered, wearing a sheepskin coat. He held a .30/.30 rifle in one hand.

"Well," he said laconically. "So where are they?"

"Looks deserted, Ellis," said one. "Except for him."

He gestured at Starky, now hanging from the limb more than standing.

"Cut me down," Starky mumbled. "For God's sake, cut me down!"

"Seen a man and a woman on the run around here, old man? or maybe a plane—a disabled or cracked-up plane—silver Cessna? Did the pilot tie you up?"

Starky shook his head.

The fat man walked over to Starky. "Who did it then? Murphy, the pilot, wasn't it?"

"Man and a woman," Starky muttered. "Cut me down."

"Bull," said the fat man, but he turned to the man called Ellis. "Would Murphy have had anyone with him?"

"Wouldn't think so—not on a run like this. Not a woman."

"He's not going to be fooling with no woman," said one of the men. "Not with all that stuff on board."

"Collins thought they'd be around here by now." Then to Starky: "Which way'd they go?"

Starky raised his head, then gestured toward the north.

"How long ago?"

"One hour, maybe more. Cut me down!"

Ellis looked at him. Then he wheeled. "I dunno— I think they're still here. Johnson—go around in back—that springhouse. Henny—the haystack. Abbie—inside."

As the men snapped at the orders, Ellis looked around him. David saw his eyes focus on the woodbin. Then the man walked toward it.

David watched him come, and his heart was beating hard.

"Not a sound!" he breathed to the women.

He worked the pistol out of his pocket and pointed it upward so that when the last log was removed from above him he could jab the pistol up and fire into the man's face.

He couldn't see the man now, but he heard the footsteps stop in front of the bin. He heard the man's rifle barrel against the wood as he lifted up the lid. David's hand trembled as he waited for the logs to be lifted out. But the man, after a long study of the bin, dropped the lid.

David eased out his breath as he watched the man walk away.

Ellis' hunched frame disappeared around the house and David heard the kitchen door bang. Now he could see only Starky and Henny, who was jabbing a pitchfork around in the haystack.

But in a few moments Ellis banged out of the house and strode up to Starky. David could see that he had a book behind his back.

"Okay, Pop," Ellis said. "Where's the woman?"

"She—she's left," Starky said. "My wife—she's gone."

"Maybe went to Piru?"

"Maybe," said Starky.

"By herself?"

Starky nodded.

Ellis slammed the book into Starky's side and the little man groaned

"She reads Braille books," shouted Ellis, "and she goes to Piru by herself?"

"They took her!" Starky whispered. "Swore they'd kill her too if I told."

Ellis smiled. "Now I think you're telling the truth for a change, you goddamn dwarf. Tell me again which way they went and it better be right!"

Starky pointed. "I tol' you right—they're headin'

for the north trail, headin' for the ranger station near Piru. And, mister, he's armed—got a pistol and stole my carbine."

"Ellis, I think Collins is workin' that area with the chopper," said one of the men. "Maybe he'll spot 'em. And Walker and the rest can't be too far away."

The fat man with the black hair came into David's view, chewing a piece of jerky. "No one in the springhouse—looked under the planks and— hey, look!" He pointed at the tethered condor across the patio. "The old pervert keeps a buzzard for a pet!"

Ellis turned to look at the bird. Henny came back from the haystack. "If that guy's in there his balls are like a sieve now."

Ellis kept staring at the condor, his thick lips curled in disbelief. The bird opened its wing to stretch, displaying the white V on the under side.

"Hey, Pop—how come you got a buzzard for a pet?" Henny said. "Them things make me puke."

"That ain't no buzzard," said Starky. "That's Blinky. He's a—"

"You're damn right it's no buzzard!" Ellis raised his rifle barrel and shot from the hip. The bullet hit the bird in the side.

At the first shot the condor gave a hop and ruffled its feathers. Then it began retching its fetid vomit, the last defense of the condor. The second shot exploded the bird's head and it fell on its side, its claws opening and closing.

You dirty bastard! welled up inside David with a burning knot of fury. *Oh, you dirty lousy bastard! I'll kill you for that!*

"Ya goddamned sumabitch!" Starky screamed. "That ain't no buzzard, that's Blinky!"

Ellis swung around and jerked the butt of the rifle up into Starky's crotch with a loud thunk. The little man jackknifed forward, and as he did Ellis brought the barrel down along the side of his head. Starky collapsed and spun slowly as he dangled from the tree by his tied hand.

"That, you dumb son of a bitches," said Ellis, "is—or was—a California condor. I just made myself a thousand bucks."

"You said we'd split!" said the fat man with the black hair.

"And so we shall," said Ellis, reloading his gun. "If you guys shape up and find the rest of them."

"Now I'm going to kill you," David said between clenched teeth.

Ellis' back was toward him. He held the pistol to the knothole and sighted through the crack. It was an easy shot, and he yearned to pull the trigger. But then, of course, they would be all annihilated. He cursed silently and lowered the pistol. He saw Ellis gesture to the other men and start across the field.

"How about the old man?" called the man, bringing up the rear.

"Like him fine where he is," said Ellis.

David watched them move across the field.

"Did they do something to Pa?" Maddy asked. "I got to go to him."

"Not yet," David ordered.

Even after the men were hidden by the tall grass, David counted to fifty. Then, before he could start to get out of the log cocoon, he saw Starky go into action. He jumped up, grabbed the branch he was attached to with both hands, and swung down with all his might. The branch cracked at the trunk. He whipped out the knife from his pants and slashed the rope that held him to the branch. He ran to the bin and threw off the logs that covered David and helped him out. The two of them then uncovered the women.

"Pa—you all right?" Maddy asked as David lifted her out.

"They shouldna oughta done that to Blinky," Starky muttered, and the way he said the words and the animal look in his eyes was chilling. He pulled the shingle from his pants. "This probably saved m'balls. Figured them piss-ants were that kind, an' they didn't disappoint me none. Now—we gotta get going fast 'fore they realize they been tricked. How much ammunition you got, Brandy?"

"One bullet."

"I'd give you my rifle" said Starky, "but I only got two shells."

He looked around him. On the side of the house hung several traps. Starky took down a large one. "If I gave you the bigger one you couldn't set it without clamps, so I'll give you the number 14 Beaver Jump. If they come after you, try slowing 'em down with this. Not going to take 'em long to figure out there's only one trail out of this valley and it ain't the direction they're headin' now. But by the time they figure it out we'll be at the top of the trail in the cave."

"The cave?" said Paige.

"Old Chumash Indian cave sitting right there. And, Brandy, in that cave I got a surprise they ain't gonna like!" The little man's eyes burned happily at the thought. "Now, let's go!"

"Me too, Pa?" Maddy asked.

"Can't leave you around here with them gorillas," said Starky.

"And Blinky?"

"He's dead, and no time for burying. Now he's carrion for feedin' somethin' else."

David was still trying to make sense of it all.

"Why in God's name did they want to kill Blinky? Why are they out to kill the rest of the condors? Like the other bunch—the man who shot the turkey vulture obviously thought he was killing a condor. Why? And who's paying them a thousand dollars a dead bird?"

"Who stands to benefit by the elimination of the condor?" Paige asked. "I have one idea and it would make sense if—"

"Better get goin'!" said Starky. "And take the Beaver Jump."

Starky slung the rusty trap over David's shoulder, and then, holding his rifle in one hand, started across the field in his crouching lope in the opposite direction from where the men had gone. The women followed as fast as they could, Maddy holding Paige's hand while David brought up the rear. Maddy stumbled and fell once; David picked her up.

Soon the field ended and the mountain began. Starky pointed out the trail snaking in and out among the boulders.

"Once you get almost up to the ridge the cave's to the right. I'll meet you there, but first I got to meander around and see what those buggers are up to."

"Take care, Pa," said Maddy.

He kissed her awkwardly.

"You too, Mad."

Then he was off in his animal-like trot. He disappeared in a few moments and they could trace his movements only by the bending ribbon of the grass across the field.

The trail was steep but not difficult, and they climbed fast.

God, David thought, what madness this all was. Two groups of a gang apparently racing each other to see how many condors they could kill, and Paige, Starky and Maddy caught in the middle of it!

"Rest," Paige gasped. "Need to stop."

"The cave," said Maddy. "It's not far now. I'm sure it's not far."

But they stopped and David glanced down at the distant valley; already they were so high up that the yellow airplane looked like a model next to a toy barn.

Then his eye caught movement far down at the bottom of the trail. It was the four men.

"Come on," he said. There was no point in telling the women yet; they had a mile lead on the men.

When they were halfway to the top, David stopped again and looked back. He could see only three of them now—strung out, coming along fast, pistols drawn, looking around boulders before advancing.

"They're coming," he said flatly.

They started off again, but this time David stayed behind the women.

When he next looked back down he could see only two of the pursuing men—the fat man in front, and fifty feet behind, the tall one called Ellis. Perhaps the other two were following false leads off the trail.

Soon the ridge was only a few hundred yards away—a jagged haven. But now when David looked down he caught a glimpse of a matted black head and he could see that the fat man—and the fat man alone—was closing in on them dangerously fast.

"Keep going!" David commanded the women. They were panting hard—Maddy less than Paige—but they could make the ridge if they kept going. He watched as they disappeared around the corner. Then he went a few feet back down the trail and peered over a boulder. Through the brush he could now see the fat man clearly, his belly heaving, his hand with the pistol extended, his powerful legs like khaki sausages pumping him steadily forward. Ellis and the others were nowhere in sight.

David slung the heavy trap off his shoulder. He found an almost level spot, a narrow hollow between two boulders. He stood on the trap, one foot on each spring handle, and the saw-tooth jaws, released from the spring tension, fell open limply. He bent down and gingerly lifted the dollar-sized pan until it caught against the trigger. Then he cautiously stepped off the trap. The trigger mechanism held. He knelt down and scooped up a handful of dust and twigs and he sprinkled them over the pan and the jaws. Another scoop covered the springs. It was ready.

He was tempted to peer around the boulder to see how near the quarry was, but there was no time. Drawing his pistol, he ran ten feet up the trail and crouched behind a rock.

He heard the man crashing up the trail, breathing hard. He couldn't be more than twenty feet from the trap—now fifteen—now twelve. David held his pistol ready and waited.

David never heard the trap go off. All he heard was a cry, like that of a fur-bearing animal. David pushed himself up over the rock to see the man on the ground, writhing and gagging and clutching at the trap that had exploded upward, slamming shut just above his ankle. Blood spurted over the trap; the leg was clearly broken. David started to turn to go up the trail after the women. Then he saw a pistol the man had dropped. He ran back down to get it.

"Help me!" screamed the fat man. "Help me, oh God!"

He screamed again, his bloody hands going to his leg and up over his face and pounding the ground and then back down to his leg. "Help me!"

David grabbed the pistol. He hesitated. The man was helpless now—he could be let out of the trap. Or put him out of his misery with a shot. David moved forward uncertainly, and as he did he heard a voice say:

"Hold it right there, you son of a bitch!" Ellis, the tall man, stepped onto the trail from behind a boulder, his rifle at waist level. "And drop it."

David's grip on the pistol loosened until the gun dropped from his fingers and slid down the hill.

The man on the ground whimpered, "Ellis—God—help me! Ellis—"

"Sure, Sammy, sure," Ellis whispered soothingly. He stepped toward David, smiling. "But first I get this monkey."

David tensed.

Ellis stepped forward, raising his rifle with care.

As he began his second step a silvery flash, like a glint from a necklace, flickered below the man's chin; a second later a thread-thin red line appeared around his neck. Then his head flopped back as though it were hinged, and suddenly his throat looked like a watermelon with a wedge cut from it. Blood spurted out over his chest. He convulsed and sagged to his knees. A final spasm jerked him backward, and the wind from his lungs whined as it sprayed the blood from his throat.

Starky was behind him. Panting hard, he wiped the knife blade on his jeans. He stared down at the body. "Should have been here quicker, Brandy. But one fella back there—he was foxy. Hard to get around him."

David stared down at the corpse draining itself at his feet. He whispered, "Jesus—"

"He ain't gonna kill no more Blinkys."

The fat man moaned. He whimpered and

sobbed, "Oh, God—Oh, God . . ."

"This man's suffering," said David, still stunned by Starky's act.

Starky stepped over the corpse and came up behind the man in the trap. He reached out with his left hand, grabbed his hair firmly, jerked the head back, and the knife in his right hand slashed across the man's throat. The whimpering turned into a gurgle and the man pitched forward on his face.

"Not any more he ain't."

David stared, whitefaced, first at Starky and then at the new victim.

"Brandy, you're pukin' green," the little man grunted, wiping the knife and returning it to the sheath inside his pants. "What'd you want to do— leave him out here for the cougars to finish off? Or carry him on your back up the hill?"

David kept staring at the bodies.

"Better catch up with the girls," said Starky.

Numbly, David pointed down the trail. "What about the other two men?"

"I'll try leadin' em off the scent." Starky gestured down at the meadow below them. "Then I'm gonna go back and hide the airplane."

"Hide it?" asked David. "Hide a plane?"

"Cover it over with hay."

"With that little bit of hay?"

Starky grinned. "Ain't gonna be but a little bit of airplane. After I set fire to it."

"No," said David. "Don't burn it."

"You know how to fly?"

"Not for twenty years. But we may have to."

"Okay. You get to the cave—it's just around the corner and up to that ridge." He hesitated. "Oh— say, Brandy. Take care of Maddy."

"You take care of yourself, Starky."

Silently they shook hands. Then Starky turned

and trotted down the trail and was quickly
swallowed up by the boulders.

David pushed back up the trail to where the
women were resting. It was clear they could not go
much farther; but then, if Starky was right, there
was not much farther to go.

Less than two hundred yards above them was the
ridge. And unless Starky was lying or wrong, just
below that ridge would be the cave. And the surprise
that he promised would be in it. It had better be a
good one.

"One last push," he said. He took Paige's hand
and she reached out to Maddy. He dug his feet into
the dirt and started to drag them forward up the
trail.

"Look there!" said Paige, suddenly pointing
down in the valley. There, across the meadow, in the
opposite direction from the way he and Paige had
descended, they could see five men coming fast on
horseback and even at this distance he could
recognize the fat man as the one the motorcycle
gang had called Walker. It was all beginning to
make some sort of crazy sense. Went back to
Collins, the ranger. Somehow he must be behind
this. Was he perhaps head of this condor-killing
ring, and if so why? And where was Collins himself?
One of the new gang had said he was in a helicopter
looking for them. David scanned the empty sky.

"Come on!" he said between clenched teeth to the
two women. "The cave—and quick!"

Chapter Nine

Another twenty minutes of labored climbing got
them to a flattened plateau. Fifty yards ahead the
trail ended abruptly at a sheer rock wall. Maddy
moved on forward, slowly sliding her feet over the
near-level ground; she was breathing heavily, her
white teeth dry against her lips. Her long hair was
damp against her forehead, her cheeks were flushed,
and her wet cotton T-shirt clung against her firm
body. She stopped abruptly and clapped her hands
twice; the sound snapped back from the cliff
sharply.

Obviously pleased by the sound of the echo, she
smiled back at Paige and David. "Here," she said.
"We're here now."

But there was no cave. Only the sudden
sandstone cliff and rocks and boulders and the

dead-end trail. David slumped against the side of the path; in spite of the heat that burned into his aching lungs, he felt the chill of fear and disappointment. Somewhere they must have taken the wrong turn.

It had been ridiculous to expect that a blind girl could lead them to a sanctuary in this vast jumble of mountain wilderness.

But Maddy turned again and walked on ahead with her graceful stride, occasionally guiding herself along the edge of the trail by running her hands lightly along the rocks at the upper side. She continued walking until she reached the cliff.

And there she vanished.

David shook his head and rubbed the sweat from his eyes. She was gone, as though by a magician's trick. There was nothing ahead but the empty trail and the great rugged cliff. For a moment he could only stare incredulously at the spot where he'd last seen her standing, expecting the mirage to disappear and make her visible again.

He stared until the trail appeared to dance in the heat; he was aware of the humming in his head and the shirring of the cicadas in the brush below. He glanced quickly back at Paige; she was curled against a rock, exhausted but all right. With a lurch he started along the plateau toward the cliff; he was almost there when Maddy miraculously reappeared in front of him.

Now David was close enough to see some of the rocks appear to undulate and flap weirdly. And he was close enough to see how the illusion had been accomplished; he could see the outline of the mouth of a cave, an area about eight feet high and five feet wide. Hanging down over the entrance were two strips of heavy canvas on which realistic rocks and boulders had been painted. Even at ten or twelve feet the eye was fooled by the camouflage.

Maddy said, "David? David, are you there?" Her eyes were amethyst now and they looked directly at his face—then to his left and to his right. "And Paige—are you all right?"

David turned and looked back down the trail; Paige was still pressed against the rock. "She's all right—just tired. I'd better help her."

As David walked back toward the exhausted woman, he looked out over the valley that dropped so sharply below him it looked almost like a papier-mâché model. It seemed impossible that the men could be far in any direction; indeed, it was most probable that the remaining Rock Hounds—and how many remained? five, six?—were already climbing the steep trail. And Starky? God alone knew where he might be and what he might be doing to lure them away from the cave's location.

The dead-end trail gave David a claustrophobic feeling, but the sun was already beginning to slide behind the great hills and the women couldn't go any farther without rest. They had no choice but to spend the night in the cave, hiding behind that clever but vulnerable canvas curtain. Still, he couldn't shake the conviction that they were finally going to be trapped and killed.

He continued down the slight decline to where Paige slept. She was half-kneeling, her arms crossed over the boulder, her head pillowed in her arms. Her blond-streaked hair was tangled and caught with bits of twigs and a leaf; there was a purplish bruise along her right cheek. Her blouse was stained and torn; her tailored beige slacks were dirty, slashed and tattered, one scabbed knee showed from a hole worn through the fabric. Her jacket with all its useless belts attached had been forgotten in the escape from the house that morning; her ridiculous safari hat with its badger tuft lost somewhere near the ranger station.

As David gazed down at her he suddenly felt a surge of affection for her. She'd claimed she wasn't a quitter and she'd proven herself, taking far more punishment than David because she was not as tall as he and therefore was more vulnerable to the tearing brush. And she was not prepared for the violence of this terrain, either physically or by experience. He thought back to when he'd first seen her step from the pickup truck—for all the world like a high-fashion model prepared to pose for some on-location shots for *Vogue* or *Harper's Bazaar*. He could barely remember what he'd felt about her then; now he felt pride—mixed with the kind of love he felt for all young, helpless things.

Looking fondly down at her as she slept, he noticed there was a greenish tint to her light skin; it was just evident beneath her eyes and around her lips. She was breathing rapidly—almost panting— and there were tiny pearls of perspiration on her upper lip. Beneath her darker eyelids he saw the flick-flick of rapid eye movement.

Leaning down, he gently laid the palm of his hand across her forehead; it was cool, damp— almost clammy—to the touch.

Suddenly she stirred; then she jerked upright and, without opening her eyes, began flailing wildly at David. "Get back! Go back! Stay away—don't come nearer! Go back!"

David knelt and swung his arms about her and held her secure against his chest to stop her furious punching.

When at last she opened her eyes they were glazed, wild and without comprehension. He said,

"It's all right, Paige...everything's all right...."

She sobbed a great breath of air, then rested her head against his shoulder. Still he rubbed the back of her tangled hair with clumsy gentleness as he continued to soothe her.

When she spoke again, she spoke into his chest, but her voice, though soft, was crisp and controlled. "Christ, what a dream! Ungodly nightmare—I can still smell them burning."

"Who?"

"The dogs. Pets of mine, but they were more like wolves—great, huge timber wolves. And they were trying to come to save me. But something was burning underneath the ground they had to cross to get to me—like a peat fire under the dry grass. And it was so hot they couldn't make it, and they would sink down and lie on that baking earth and look hopelessly at me with their wonderful brown eyes. And then they'd start to burn—still alive and watching me. They began to smell and their hair came loose from their bodies. And their eyes smoked dry...still looking at me. Then the ants came and crawled up their nostrils and over their eyes and their bodies burst and split open. And another wolf began to come to save me from the other side and I tried to make him stay back. The ants were on my face then and crawling to my nose and there was nothing I could do about it and—and—"

Her voice trailed off. He held her moments longer before he released her. Studying her face with concern, he reached across and felt her brow again. It felt more normal to the touch and the greenish cast was less noticeable.

"How do you feel?" he asked.

"Like a million," she said weakly.

"No—really, how do you feel?"

"About the way I look, I suppose," she murmured.

He helped her to stand up.

They were still struggling when an unearthly whine came from the valley below; a scream of pain too high-pitched to have come from a human throat. Then a series of muted explosions that quickly settled to a steady *whack-whack-whack-whack*.

They stared dumbly at each other: the helicopter!

Without a word he grabbed her hand and they began running clumsily along the plateau toward the hidden cave. The fifty yards seemed to stretch out interminably and with every step David felt the nightmarish certainty that the copter was climbing directly up their backs; that they were only running in place and would never reach the cave.

Finally, gasping hot air into his lungs and half dragging Paige behind him, David made it to the cave and pushed their way inside.

Paige sank to the sandy ground. After the bright afternoon sun, the interior of the cave appeared totally black; only faint streaks and blotches of light managed to filter through the canvas. The air in the cave was dankly cool and there was a bitter smell to it like old sulphur or nitro. The odor transported him back to Big Timber, Montana—the Fourth of July at the Rodeo grounds, the smell of a hundred cap pistols being fired, fuseless firecrackers bent into "sizzlers," and the crackly "Red Devils" you stepped on.

Maddy's voice floated lightly and hollowly from the dark interior. "David—Paige—come closer to the fire. It'll be warmer soon."

"Where are you?" David asked. His voice was taken by the darkness and then bounced gently back from a long series of invisible walls.

"Sorry," the blind girl said. "I forgot you can't see. Wait there a minute."

The irony of it jolted David into a sharp realization of the world in which Maddy had learned to live. Here the blind could see and those who saw were blind.

A second later he heard the rattle of a match box and the scratch-snap of a wooden kitchen match. A dull gold reflected off the wall and Maddy came around a bend in the cave, carrying a kerosene lantern.

David helped Paige up and they followed the blind girl to where a freshly started fire glowed. Chunks of ancient slag walled the fire; an old iron grilling was set across one corner. Two nail kegs were drawn up near to the slag piles; a tarp, blankets and burlap bags lay stacked along a side of the cave wall.

David led Paige to the pile of gunnysacks where she sank with a groan of fatigue. He sidled over to a nail keg and sat on it. Dropping his sweaty face in his hands, he felt himself sliding into a near coma of fatigue: images swirled in his head as though in a flu fever.

He half-dreamed again the terrible violence: the two men slaughtered by Starky. Shivering, he once again saw the blood spurt from the severed necks, and the man he himself had killed with the makeshift crossbow a lifetime of terrors ago. Another human life wasted. What a travesty—that the condors, at the top of the death list themselves, should be the cause of this terrible extermination of human life.

Surprisingly, David had witnessed very little personal violence in his life—mostly some distant skirmishes in battlefields viewed through a telescopic lens when he was a combat photographer at the bitter end of the Korean War. And the picador killed in front of him in the Malaga arena. Yet somehow the senseless death of Blinky, a grotesque pet condor, was more poignant and scarring than the calculated killing of the three brutish men who had died in their attempt to destroy him.

Shortly—though he felt he'd dreamt an eternity—David forced himself to lift his head and study the cave about him. Little by little the walls came into focus as his eyes grew accustomed to the lantern light. Then the fire began to flare and he saw a hulking giant spring up black and menacing against the ghost-yellow wall directly in front of him—his own double shadow cast by the flickering kerosene light and the glowing fire.

Aloud he said, "The copter. They've sent the helicopter to catch us." He listened intently, but the heavy curtain blocked all sounds from outside the cave.

"They won't find us," Maddy said. "In the days before the slide closed the trail, Pa and I hid in here and men walked right on by not twenty feet away. Never suspected."

David thought of the painted curtain again. "It's a great job of camouflage," he said. "Did Starky do it?"

"I did it," she said. "I learned how to do it studying art in Chicago."

He rose and looked around the cave as Maddy moved to his side. "Originally this was a Chumash Indian cave," she said. "Then, a long time ago, the miners moved in and used it for storage. They drilled a lot of shafts that connect to it, and many others that stop and start and don't make sense anymore."

The cave appeared fathomless to David. The wall in front of him was perhaps ten to twelve feet away; the rounded wall behind him dissolved into near-darkness. Above, the gothic roof undulated like a sea turned upside down till it dissolved from lack of light. Now he saw two tunnels join the cave atrium, and on the floor rusty iron rails, small and narrow 8-gauge rails, as though for a miniature train. Dimly, he could perceive some sort of a vehicle on one set of rails—it was a crudely constructed miner's barrow made of metal and wood. Then, barely visible, he was able to make out the wheels underneath a heavy tarpaulin tied over the rig. The diminutive rail line ran the length of the cave, past the fire and to the camouflaged mouth in front.

He began an exploratory walk deeper into the cave.

David asked, "Do you have another light I could use? I'd like to look around."

Maddy turned and went to a barrel, struck a match in front of a second kerosene lamp. Fumbling only slightly, she lifted the glass chimney from the lamp, touched the match to the wick and replaced the chimney; and all the while David marveled at her sense of place and act of blind prestidigitation. She passed her hand over the top of the chimney, feeling the amount of heat the lamp poured out the top. With her free hand still waving lightly above the glass, she adjusted the wick until it burned cleanly and offered the lighted lamp to David.

Suddenly she stiffened and turned her head up and abruptly to one side. For a moment David stared, then he heard it. Outside the cave, beyond the canvas curtain, came the muted sound of the helicopter's motor: *whump-whump-whump-whump.*

Closer and closer it came; for countless minutes it seemed glued to the top of the cave. And then abruptly the sound diminished and vanished.

"Jesus!" David sighed.

Maddy smiled brightly at him. "I told you—it works."

Picking up the lamp, he began walking slowly toward the rear of the cave. With each step the yellow kerosene flame bowed back and forth and the cave appeared to dip and swing in the dancing light.

Then he came to a large niche crammed with ancient supplies and equipment like the backroom of an old country hardware store. There were large wooden boxes, coils of rope, bales of rusted wire, barrels, sacks and pulleys, picks and shovels, and stakes and crowbars—all orange-brown with rust. The faded, dust-covered letters DYN----E were still visible on one crate. Next to it was a battered wooden box with a T-shaped plunger that he recognized as an exploder, exactly the type and vintage his father had used to blow up stumps and crumble great boulders back when he widened the road leading to their ranch outside Big Timber, Montana. And there was a cigar box filled with moldy-green brass dynamite caps, each little cylinder wrapped round with its two wires; nearby was a big coil of light insulated wire, its stripped copper ends attached to the screws on the exploder, all covered with the green mushroom of corrosion.

A dented tin bucket was quarter-filled with a jumble of old bullets, their blunt black lead noses powdered gray. David sifted through them with his fingers. They were all obsolete and too fat to fit the 9 mm Luger. Bitterly he reflected he'd be in great shape if they were still fighting the Civil War.

Then it occurred to him that with all this

ammunition there had to be some guns of the proper caliber—maybe even one that was capable of working. They could polish the shells so they'd fit into the chamber. The possibility of being able to at least put up a decent fight started new adrenaline through him and he felt less tired.

"Maddy," he called.

Her figure appeared to float ghostlike from the gloom into the light of his lantern.

"Where'd your father put the rifles—the pistols—"

Maddy shook her head. "There never were rifles or pistols. Miners must have taken them when they went."

David felt the spirit draining out of him.

Then, almost incidentally, as though she were changing the subject, Maddy said, "Of course, there's Pa's cannon!"

David stared at her uncomprehendingly.

She moved past him and felt her way along the wall until she came to the cart on the tracks that ran along the center of the cave. A green tarpaulin covered the vehicle's bulging cargo.

As David walked up behind her with the lamp, Maddy was pulling at the corner of the canvas. "Pa's special pride."

When she lifted the tarp, shiny machinery gleamed in the lantern light. Another fold of the canvas revealed a twin-barreled .50-caliber machine gun glinting a crisp greenish black.

It took David several seconds to bridge the gap from the bucket of nineteenth-century bullets to this World War II artillery. Then he realized this was the gun missing from the mount in the crashed bomber.

Maddy smiled. "He comes up here and oils and fusses with it regular. Been doing it ever since before I can remember. Does it look all right?"

David whistled softly. "It looks as though it had been built yesterday." He fingered the belt loaded with brass shells and the trigger mechanism.

Maddy nodded. "Pa always kept it ready. He figured they'd be coming any time. Swore he wasn't going to let them take him back alive."

"Doesn't that seem a little excessive? Lots of men have gone AWOL in a lot of wars. They're not going to kill him."

"He's been getting stranger these last years. At first it was only the MPs, then it was the whole Navy. Now it's pretty near everybody is out after him."

"But still—"

"There was more to it than just AWOL," Maddy admitted hesitantly. "He got into a fight with a couple of MPs—off duty. Pa allows as how he was drunk—real drunk. Kneewalkin', commode-huggin' drunk, as he calls it. Claims it was a fair fight. But when he woke up one of the men was dead and the other bleeding something fierce. Pa didn't wait to see if he'd get a fair trial. Been hiding out ever since."

David sighed. Given the circumstances, he suspected Starky'd probably figured right. Under wartime regulations they probably would have executed him; at best he might have gotten life.

David continued staring at the weapon: the thing had to weigh twice as much as Starky. "How did he manage to get it up here?"

"Brought it up on the rigging."

"The rigging?"

Maddy flipped the canvas over the machine gun again. "I'll show you."

She walked up the cave, guiding herself by the feel of the rails, and David followed. They passed

the fire and pile of tarps, sacks and blankets where
Paige now slept, one of the sacks pulled across her
shoulders.

Maddy pushed through the canvas curtain. It
was getting darker by the minute now and the sky
looked like rain. David glanced at his watch. It was
stopped and the crystal had been spider-webbed
somewhere along the line. He guessed it was about
six o'clock. There was no sign of the men or of
Starky. Maddy pointed back up to the right. There
were three posts, as thick as telephone poles, ten feet
high, lashed together at their tops tepee style and
solid in the side of the mountain.

Secured to them was a cable that ran down the
hill for almost half a mile, propped up at intervals by
other posts. The sagging cable cleared the rocks by
only a few feet, but then as the hill grew steeper the
cable was as high as fifty feet off the ground. There
was a platform, hung from two rusty wheels,
tethered near the first and highest post. There were
pulleys and a coil of rope hung on that post.

"Anything large, barrels or whatever, Pa loads
on the platform way down there. Then he hitches
the mule to the rope on the pulley and up it comes.
The miners set it up first, Pa just repaired what they
left that was wore out or rotten."

"It makes one hell of a funicular," David said.

"It works."

The day was growing cold. A sharp gust of wind
had blown the lantern out. David took one last look
at the valley and saw no signs of movement.
Turning, he took Maddy's arm and they went
inside.

The fire had consumed the original kindling, and
starter logs had begun to settle into a softening
glow. Earlier, David had noticed a stacked pile of

logs along the near wall. He made several trips to the pile, building a steady-burning fire to provide both warmth and a cook-fire.

Maddy had opened another box and taken out a frying pan, a tin of flour and strips of dried meat. Paige stirred and continued to sleep. Watching Maddy, David had to force himself to believe she couldn't see; she moved with such ease and self-assurance, a half-smile about her lips.

After a moment, he relighted the second lamp and made his way toward the back of the cave to where it divided. He followed the largest tunnel past other shafts that yawned briefly in the dim light before swallowing it with their blackness. When the roof of his tunnel dipped abruptly, David set the lantern on the floor of the cave and urinated against the wall. Afterward, he tried to work his way further back, crouching beneath the ever-closer sandstone ceiling. It seemed impossible that this cave didn't come out some other place on the mountain, but the cave floor dropped off steeply; drops of water dripped on his neck and distantly he heard the rush of water in the darkness ahead.

Hunched over awkwardly, David turned and began to work his way back up the cave. When he got to the fire, the frying pan was sizzling on the grating and Maddy was kneeling beside a stone, slapping dough into round flat cakes.

Maddy raised her head at the sound of his return and said, "You're back."

"I was looking for another way out."

"There is," she said. "But it's too dangerous."

She laid the strips of dried meat in the center of the cakes and wrapped them into tortillas. "Venison," she said.

David tongued the inside of his mouth. "Damned hungry," he said. "And thirsty."

Maddy arose without a word and touched her way around to an oil drum set against the bend in the cave's wall. Water dripped from the side of the cave with an arhythmic *plip-plop* into the barrel; the overflow slid across the worn edge of the container and disappeared into a crack in the cave floor. Taking a tin cup from a hook hanging on the side of the drum, Maddy dipped fresh water into the cup, swirled it about, and tossed the contents against the wall where it washed down into the same natural drain. Then she filled it again, brought the cup to David. He reached out and gratefully took a drink. The water was so metallically cold it seemed to ring against his teeth.

When David had finished the whole cupful without a pause, Maddy said, "There's more if you'd like it. And Pa's got some medicinal here, too."

Before David could respond, a pair of shots crackled in the valley below. Then a third shot. Then silence. They got him, David thought. They got Starky. And he prayed he was mistaken.

Maddy sat quietly for a second before she said, "Pa's all right. He can take care of himself."

"Sure he can," David said a little too loudly. "I've never seen a man who handles himself the way he can."

"What is it? What's happening?" Paige was struggling to sit up; fighting to get untangled from her covering.

"It's all right, Miss Evans," Maddy said.

"Christ, what's going on?" She was sitting upright now, staring wide-eyed and uncomprehending at the fire. After a minute she blinked, then dropped her face into her hands with a sob. "God, a nightmare. I thought it was a nightmare. But it wasn't, was it?"

David went to the water barrel, filled the cup and

went to kneel beside the confused woman.

"Here," he said. "Drink this."

She took the cup in her hands like a small child and drank the water in sips. David lifted one of the sacks and laid it gently across her shoulders like a burlap poncho.

Then he slipped his fingers around the butt of the Luger in his pocket and stood up. "I guess I'll go outside and look around a bit."

Maddy stared up in his direction for a long moment. "Pa always says to be careful going out after dark—light from the cave up here's going to shine a long way across the valley."

David nodded. "I'll be careful."

"What's going on?" Paige asked suddenly. "What're you both talking about? Stop treating me like a goddamned child!"

"It's all right," Maddy said. "There was just a little shooting outside."

"Oh, shit!" Paige exploded. "Just a little shooting—that's all! Just a little simple everyday shooting." Then she dropped her face in her hands.

Maddy said, "It's all right, Miss Evans. Everything's all right."

"Please don't call me Miss Evans."

David stopped at the canvas curtains, cautiously pushed one portion aside and slid through the narrow gap.

Another shot rang out from somewhere far across the valley.

Holding his breath, David waited for a crackling barrage to return the fire. The silence lasted interminably until all seemed silent. And only then David moved to the edge of the trail and peered into the darkening valley.

Purple shadows flooded the deepest canyons; gentian violet stained the upper hills; spoils of dark greens and hot yellows washed the last of the sunlit rises. The sky was already a faded blue dimming to night, and the evening winds were still. From David's perch above all that stretched below, Starky's Valley might have looked the same in all of the countless eons that had passed before.

He sighed, turned and made his way up to the canvas, slipped inside and back to the fire.

Paige stood up. "I'm afraid I have to go powder my nose or something."

David got up and reached for the kerosene lamp. "It's a big place," he said. "I'll show you the way."

"I'll manage," she said and took the lantern from him and walked shakily toward the back of the cave.

Maddy said, "Some medicinal?"

"It's time," David agreed.

She got up and took the cup from the water barrel, then felt for a small keg on a nearby rock. Turning the spout, she filled the cup with clear liquid and brought it to David.

The liquor smelled bad and it was bitter. Having learned from last night's experience, David sipped it cautiously.

The fire had begun to burn down. Taking Maddy's hand, he placed the half-empty cup in it, then fetched two more logs and used them as pokers to rearrange the already burning wood before he added them to the blaze. The disturbance created a brief shower of sparks and a billow of smoke.

David coughed. "Smoke," he explained. "I'm surprised it's not worse in here."

Maddy pointed to the ceiling directly above the fire. At the very top of the arching stone David saw the end of a pipe poking down into the cave. Through it he glimpsed a circle of evening sky and then a faint early star.

"Your father thought of everything."

Maddy shook her head. "The miners. That pipe has always been here."

As he moved back to sit on the barrel, David realized he'd begun to worry about Paige. God knows, it was a place one could get lost—perhaps for days.

"Tell me about your mother."

Maddy shrugged. "She's dead now. They said it was cirrhosis. She was from France. Brest. Her parents kept a little café. She wanted to be a great singer or artist, but she wasn't good enough so she worked at what she could. Mostly she was a maid. She always wanted me to be an artist, too."

"How did you manage to get to art school?"

"Once when she ran away from Pa, she worked for some nice people in Chicago. Instead of paying her, they paid my art lessons. She wanted me to study in Paris someday."

A light glowed from the lower end of the cave and shortly Paige appeared. She had straightened her hair and arranged her ragged clothes as neatly as possible.

Setting the lamp on its ledge, she said, "A city girl could sure get lost in a joint like this."

Maddy said, "Paige—would you like a bit of Pa's medicinal?"

"I don't think so, Maddy."

But the blind girl was already filling the cup. "It'll perk you up. Then the food will be ready."

Paige took the proffered cup and drank quickly from it. She gulped dryly for an instant before she could expel her breath, cough and gasp, "Thank you—I'm perked. Lordy, am I ever perked!"

David took the cup from her and sipped at the remaining liquid as Maddy kneeled by the fire. She placed an ancient frying pan on the grating and waited until the oil began to sizzle, then dropped the enchilada cakes neatly in the pan where they sputtered angrily. Paige and David watched with a hypnotized kind of fascination.

Abruptly Paige turned to David, "Why? Why do they have to kill us? Why can't they just leave us alone—we never did anything to them!"

Though her teeth were clenched and her voice soft, there was an unnatural intensity in her tone. David reached the cup across toward her.

Paige rejected it with an angry wave of her hand. "If I'm going to be hounded to death, at least I want to know why!"

"They're murderers—we're witnesses." He patted his pocket containing the roll of film.

"Well—hell, I'm not going to tell! I'll sign a piece of paper—whatever. They don't have to kill me!"

Maddy turned the enchiladas that snapped at each other in the fying pan. "Pa always said they'd come. Said once they found Starky's Valley they was bound to come and bound to ruin it. Bound to build roads and houses and bridges and pave it all in cement just like they did everyplace else. He got the cave ready for when they come to the valley."

Paige laughed bitterly. "I don't quite see this as the ideal location for Peter Stuyvesant Village the Second. Condominiums and all. Hey—they could call them condorminiums." This struck her funny and she laughed too loudly. "Condorminiums!"

Maddy lifted two of the enchiladas and laid one each in battered but clean tin plates which she offered to David and Paige. The third she put on a small shinglelike board for herself; the last she left in the frying pan. "Pa will be hungry when he comes," she explained to no one in particular. "He'll want his medicinal and he'll be hungry."

"Maybe not a Stuyvesant Village," said David, "but Starky's right about something. There are too many people involved, too well organized, too much equipment not to have some plan behind it. God knows what that plan's all about, though."

"Money," Paige said flatly. "It always comes down to money."

"Money for what? They can't do anything with this place—it's a sanctuary. It's forbidden by law."

Paige smiled wryly. "A sanctuary for what, David?"

"The condors, for God's sake!"

"And if all the condors suddenly happen to wake up dead?"

"That's a little excessive, don't you think? To wipe an entire species off the face of the earth just for a chunk of godforsaken land?"

"I don't know." She shrugged. "But you might ask any American Indian you happen to run into."

David bit down hard on the last of his enchilada and chewed, staring silently into the fire. And he thought of the light plane Starky had told him about that had crashed recently with a load of deer carcasses. Could the plane have been seeding the hills with poisoned venison for the condors? The idea was monstrous.

Paige said, "Maddy, let's clean up."

"You just rest yourself. I know where things go."

Paige hesitated before she accepted the girl's refusal. Then she stood up. "God, I'm really wiped out."

"There's two tarps and two blankets and the sacks," Maddy said. "Pa and I put one tarp on the ground, then the sacks for softness. We put the blankets and the other tarp over us—it works out pretty good."

She had risen as she talked, and started around the fire toward the bedding, but David stopped her. "I'll handle that."

After Paige had lain down on a side of the makeshift bed, David covered her gently with one of the blankets and the tarp.

"Lord, I ache," she sighed.

He leaned over and kissed her softly on the forehead. "Sleep. It'll be better in the morning."

"Mmmmmmm." And she was asleep.

As David stood up again he realized how much he, too, ached. When he returned to the fire, Maddy had nearly completed the necessarily limited kitchen chores.

"Maddy, if there's enough of that medicinal left, I'd sure like to help myself to another cup."

Her smile flashed in the firelight. "One thing's always certain—wherever Pa's at, there's going to be plenty of medicinal."

The cup was nearly full when he heard the scream. Even though it was not close by, the sound was so startling he jerked about, spilling half the contents of the cup. By the time he had refilled the cup and turned the spigot off, he had identified the cry.

"Mountain lion?" he asked.

She nodded.

"Not one of your father's imitations?" He sat on the barrel again.

"That was a real one. Used to be quite a few; not many anymore. I raised an orphaned cub two years ago; his name was Gato. I loved him, but Pa made me let him take Gato way back up the mountains so he couldn't find his way home. Said he was needed to keep his tribe going."

She sat quietly on her barrel, her hands folded in her lap. Again David wondered at her amazing endurance. Of course, she was young and conditioned to the outdoors. And she had begun this day's climb rested—unlike Paige and himself, who had already been bruised and badly fatigued from the previous days. Still, it had been a long day and a hard climb.

Maddy sighed. "I wonder if he remembers me anymore . . . Gato."

"I got some great photos of two mountain lions last week," David said. "They were mating. Awkward and clumsy, the way he mounts her. But still nice—and somehow very sensual. He sort of massages her hips with his back feet to reassure her." He yawned—the medicinal was getting to him. "To tell her he's not trying to kill her. Great shots—" He stifled another yawn with his hand. Then he remembered with a spasm that these films had been lost with the rest. He told her briefly about how the case had fallen into the river.

Maddy said, "Pa will find them. Pa can find anything—whether it's lost or not."

His hopes rose briefly. "The case is watertight—it'll float. And aluminum, so it'll be easy to spot." Then he felt the irony—sure, the case might be safe, but it was unlikely any of them would survive to look for it.

Maddy said, "David, I've been thinking about what we were talking about before. About Them—about how they maybe want to do things up here. Build houses and dams and all those things. And I was thinking, maybe that's all right. I mean, maybe it's selfish for just Pa and me and the big birds to have all this beautiful land and air and sky just for ourselves."

"Good God, Maddy! These aren't just any old birds. If they die, there won't be any more like them in the whole world. That's important—terribly important."

"People are important, too," she said simply.

He had to think for a moment. How to explain

the ecological interdependence of all things that live, great or small. Instead he said:

"If I don't crash pretty damned soon, I'm going to fall on my face."

Before they joined Paige under the tarp, David added more logs to the fire, banking them against the night.

After he had slid in beside Paige, Maddy came to lie next to him.

"David?" she whispered.

"Maddy?"

"You've been to Paris?"

"Yes."

"Tell me about it," she said like a child asking for a bedtime story. "My mother made it sound so—so magical."

He tried to remember the real Paris he had known for a summer so long ago, not the Paris of the movies and the novels of the twenties. It had been a good three months. He and Elaine were on their honeymoon—she had gone to the Cordon Bleu cooking school and had learned almost nothing because the classes were conducted in French. He had gone to the Julien Art Academy, thinking he might become an artist. But then he bought his first Leica and discovered he was born with the feel to be a first-rate photographer and not a second-rate painter. And they had eaten rabbit nearly every day because it was so cheap even though it distressed them both to think of eating the nice bunnies. And the dirty little café where Hemingway was said to have met Gertrude Stein and the restaurant where they ate eels without knowing it and liked them and the afternoons in the Bois, and the marvelous Gauguin which nobody else ever seemed to have noticed in the Jeu de Paume.

"Tell me about Paris, David!"

"Ah, Paris. That's a big order. Where to start. Big—a big city. Trees. Beautiful. Taxis. Noise. Old buildings."

"And the girls?"

"Chic—very made up."

"And the men?"

"Short—very lecherous."

"And the Eiffel Tower?"

"Very tall."

"And the Arc de Triomphe?"

"Very big."

"And the restaurants?"

"Very small."

"And the Louvre?"

"I will describe every single painting in the Louvre for you," he said drowsily. "But not tonight."

"Mama wanted me to see all the paintings in the Louvre. You see, when she died—my eyes—my eyes were all right."

"They will be all right again, Madelaine," he murmured. "I swear it."

He wanted to tell her more about Paris, about their dreary apartment on the Left Bank, about the tiny kitchen with a Bunsen burner for a stove. He wanted to tell her about the kitchen in his house in Connecticut, a big modern kitchen which was really part library; he wanted to tell her about his dog Grover; he wanted to tell her about Dr. Barkin, who might be able to fix her vision; about the retarded boy who was his son; about the dull ache of loneliness he'd endured since his wife's death.

He hadn't meant to go to sleep. And he didn't know how many sleeping hours later, but the next thing he felt was a hand around his throat and another over his mouth.

Chapter Ten

"You're dead," the voice hissed.

David's eyes had to blink several times before he could recognize Starky's distorted features in the dimly lit cave. Then he had to struggle to pull one gnarled hand from his throat, the other from his mouth. Suddenly the fingers relaxed and David slumped back on the makeshift bedding. Maddy and Paige had awakened and were twisting under the blankets as they attempted to sit up.

Starky crouched, straddling David_so that his weight on the tarp pressed David's back against the burlap sacks.

"Pa," Maddy said. "What're you talking crazy for?"

"By rights you ought to be dead," Starky snapped angrily. "If they'd come in the cave instead of me, you'd be dead as hammers. All of you!"

He straightened, stepped off the tarp and paced the cave. "You got no one standing watch! You got no weapons out!" He marched to the machine gun and slapped it—he was Hannibal, Bonaparte and Ulysses S. Grant. "Why ain't this out front standing ready?"

David groaned as he sat up. "Your father's right. I shouldn't have let myself fall asleep."

"You were badly wore out," Maddy said defensively. "We all were, Pa."

"Figured you ought to know better, Maddy!" Starky barked.

David stood up. "I'll go stand watch."

"You'd likely think to lock the zoo gate after the zebra was stolen. Guess I had you figured wrong, Brandy. Figured you was someone a man could trust his daughter to—not some sleeping beauty."

David said coldly, "All right, Starky, knock it off. I blew it, I admitted it and I'm sorry. But let's not spend the rest of the night bitching. There's still something we can do, so let's get started. How much time do you think we've got?"

Starky paced briefly; the tone of authority in David's voice seemed to have cut through his anger to the remaining vestiges of his Navy disciplining. "Not daylight for some time yet, Brandy," he said, subdued.

"All right, I'll go stand watch—"

Paige stood up. "No, David, let me. I haven't done a damned thing for anybody on this bloody trip except get in the way. At least I've got two good eyes"—she hesitated uncomfortably and glanced apologetically at Maddy—"and I might as well use them."

David squeezed her arm. "I don't know anybody who could have done better, Paige."

She touched his hand. Then she started for the mouth of the cave.

As they were talking, Maddy had dropped new logs on the fire, and the cave was becoming less gloomy.

David called after Paige, "Careful when you go through the curtain. Try not to let any light out." The woman paused, then slid between the canvas panels.

"Pa," Maddy said, "I got some food ready. You start eating and I'll bring the medicinal."

As Starky went to sit on the keg, David asked, "What happened out there?"

"I reconnoitered them." He bobbed his head and a quick smile of satisfaction split his lips. "Yessir, I reconnoitered them good. Sometimes as close as I am to that there wall. Could even hear them talking. Sittin' around the fire like a bunch of ol' Blinkys holdin' a council of war. Used to see a couple dozen those big birds come flockin' to a field to gather in a circle, cackle things over for a time, then fly away. That's the way they's acting—like a flock of Blinkys."

"How many?"

"Not rightly sure." With both hands Starky accepted the cup Maddy held toward him and took a long drink. Then he closed his eyes, swallowed, and finally blew out a breath of satisfaction. To David he confided, "Smells like sheep dip, don't it?"

David nodded.

"But it tastes fine, once you get past that smell." He took another sip, then reached down and bit hungrily into the last encilada.

"Did you get any kind of count at all?" David repeated.

"More'n I figured. But I never seen other than five or six all in one place at one time. They kept breakin' off, some goin' this way and some goin' that. Hard to figure."

He took another gulp and another bite before he continued. "From what I heard, they're sure we're up here someplace. They scouted the trail to Chimney, they backtrailed the way you come an' they tried North Ridge. They know this trail quits here, so they left it till last. They don't know about this here cave, but they plan to start up the trail soon's it gets light. Then they'll find their dead ones."

He finished the enchilada, washed it down with medicinal and stood up. "Once they get to nosing around here too close, they're gonna find us for sure."

David said, "I saw a bucket of shells over there— aren't there any guns to go with them?"

The little man shook his head. "No guns—except ol' Betsy." He walked over to the machine gun, wiping his hands carefully on his T-shirt before he lifted the canvas and lovingly ran his fingers over the twin barrels. "They got no idea what we got for guns. They don't know I used up my last two bullets after they shot at me—or where they figured I had ought to be. They don't know if you got any shots left in that there pistol you took away from 'em. And they don't know *nothin'* 'bout sweet ol' Betsy here. Nothin' at all! And I'll tell you what—I'll let you shoot it tomorrow!"

"Hell, Starky, I never touched one before, much less fired it."

"No trick. You just aim and pull the trigger like them guns at carnivals."

"And loading it?"

"Hell, it come all loaded and ready to go!"

"Starky, have you ever fired this gun?—or any machine gun?"

The little man looked away evasively. Then he moved quickly around to the back of the cart and began pushing. Grunting fiercely, he said, "We done too much talking already, mate. Time to move."

As he strained against the heavy mining barrow it began to move forward slightly. David took hold of one of the coupling devices on the front and pulled. Between the two of them the cart squealed along the rails to the cave's entrance.

"Hold it!" Starky stopped pushing, cautiously parted the canvas panels at the cave's mouth and looked out.

Then he turned. "Fire's low enough in here so they won't see it. Besides, we got no choice."

He beckoned silently. David gave a hard pull and the cart rolled out of the cave to the end of its rails. The clean moistness of the early morning air stung David's nostrils pleasantly after the smoky cave. A faint light was just beginning to outline the rim of the mountains across the black void below them. God—that was the very mountain that he and Paige had climbed and then descended so long ago.

Paige was standing near the edge of the shelf, looking up.

"Only thing I heard was a rustle up there a little while ago," she whispered.

"Probably an animal," he said. Tactically it would be very smart for the gang to attack unexpectedly from above, but the brush and stones made it nearly impossible for a man to get around and up without causing a lot of noise. No—they would have to try first from below.

She stared across the valley at the mountains. "Did we really come all this way, David?" she asked.

"I was thinking the same thing."

"David"—she hesitated—"there's one thing—"

"Yes?"

"If I don't make it, if something happens to me—"

"Don't talk that way—you're going to make it! We're all going to make it."

"Yes, of course," she said. "But if by some chance I don't—I want you to take charge of the magazine."

"Stop talking nonsense. Go back in the cave and help Maddy."

She smiled at him. "Maybe it was just that foolish dream."

He gave her a gentle shove and a reassuring touch on the shoulder as she turned and went into the cave.

"Gettin' light, Brandy," said Starky. He took the handle of the cart. "Let's get her to the edge—and watch yourself with that couplin' hook."

It was harder going after the wheels of the cart bumped off its rails, but the stone shelf slanted downhill and they managed to push it across the thirty-foot area. Finally David braced his feet and leaned against the cart to stop it while Starky put two rocks under the front wheels.

"There she be!" exulted the little man as he stood up and patted the metal barrow. He got behind the machine gun, took its two handles in his bony hands, pointed it down and swiveled the weapon back and forth across the mountain below them.

"I'm ready for 'em!" Starky said, his voice hoarse with excitement. "They can't get close without I can spot 'em."

"But as soon as you can see them, they're going to be able to see you."

It was growing light now and the sun's rays were visible in the direction he had assumed not long ago to be north.

He took out his knife and walked to a sumac tree growing on the side of the mountain. He grabbed a

branch and was able to bend it hard back on itself
and break it. Then he whittled through the sinewy
wood to cut it free. Dragging the heavy limb, he
walked back toward Starky. He saw Maddy step
out of the cave, and the eerie undulation of the
canvas flaps with the rocks painted on them gave
him a start once again.

"Pa, can I help?"

"Everything shipshape and at the ready," Starky
said, back in his military role. "Now, Maddy—and
you, Brandy—listen close. If somethin' bad happens
to Starky, this is what you're goin' to do." He turned
and pointed up the mountain toward the wooden
platform hanging from its overhead cable. "Quick
as foxes you take Miss Fancy Britches and get
yourselves up there. Then all you got to do is hoist
yourselves up on the carrier and loose it from the
post. That's all, the carrier does the rest. You slide
right down to the meadow—slick as a whistle.
Starky's done it lots of times—better ride than you
get at a carnival." He laughed with boyish glee at the
confession.

David shook his head. "Starky, we're not going
to leave you here."

"I could get hurt," the little man said flatly.

"Damnit, Starky—you're not going to get hurt.
Nobody's going to get hurt!" David insisted with an
assurance that sounded forced even to his own ears.

"If Starky gets hurt so he's no good, you just
leave him be," he said firmly. "Brandy, I want you to
promise. You get Maddy out of here."

David shook his head. "Even if we did manage to
get to the meadow without you—what then? We
can't outrun them any longer. And we can't hide—
there's too many of them, not even counting the
helicopter. We've got to fight it out right here—all
of us."

Starky thrust his jaw out and jabbed David in the chest with his index finger. "I'll tell you what you're goin' to do, Brandy! I'll tell you, by damn!" He continued to stab David's chest. "You'll fly out—that's what! You-all just jump in that plane they left by the house—then you fly out."

"For Christ's sake, man! I haven't flown for twenty years."

Maddy hissed sharply. "I heard something—" She swung her arm around to point down the mountain to the left of the trail. David immediately grabbed the branch, dragged it the remaining feet to heave it in front of the machine gun. It was large enough so that the spread of its leafy branches concealed the gun as well as Starky, who had ducked down behind it to clutch the triggered handles.

"Go back, Maddy!" David said in a low but urgent tone. "Back in the cave! And keep Paige in there with you."

Crouching behind a boulder, David pulled the Luger with its single bullet from his pocket. A brush snapped to his left; a dislodged rock rattled then crashed down the mountainside farther to the right. The sound of the falling rock died away and all was silent until David began to hear the sound of his own pulse pound behind his ears.

And then, a hundred feet down the cliff, Walker himself appeared. Slowly he drew himself from the ground to his full height like a hairless grizzly rising on its hind legs.

"Brand!" he bellowed.

David held his breath and waited. The man's grotesque features were mercilessly etched in the morning light—the lid of the destroyed eye sunk deep into its socket, the zipperlike scar riding down his scalp and across his face to the corner of his

mouth, the white stubble that stopped abruptly at
the edges of lake-shaped patches of scar tissue. An
oversized pistol was snugged into his plaster
encased hand.

Walker's voice boomed out again: "You're
cornered, Brand!" The words echoed back.

When he called out again the tone of his voice
had changed to one of gruff bargaining. "Be
realistic, Brand. We know you're out of shells.
Maybe you got one left—maybe two, is all."

He waited; David waited.

"We don't want no more killing, Brand. But one
way or another, we gotta have that film." Walker
took a step up the cliff. Then two other men flanking
Walker showed themselves. Another stepped out
from behind a tree. All three had rifles trained
toward the ledge. David waited for others to appear;
nervously he glanced up the mountain behind him
and saw no signs of activity.

He looked at Starky. The little man's face was
skeletally taut and his hands were trembling on the
handles of the machine gun—but, David felt, far
more in eagerness than fear. He signaled Starky by
pressing a finger to his lips and waited until the sign
was acknowledged by a quick nod.

When he peered down the cliff again, the four
men were standing motionless. But they were closer.
Somehow they had each managed to ooze a step or
two up the cliff. David pushed the Luger forward
toward the edge; the temptation to chance one
careful shot at the middle of Walker's gut was
becoming uncontrollable.

Two of the riflemen eased down on their knees
and worked their way another few feet up the cliff.
The advance was slow, but it was relentless.

David inched the Luger still closer to the edge
and pressed his way around the protective boulder.

It would not have been an especially difficult shot with a rifle, or even with Elaine's long-barreled Magnum. The closer he brought himself to risking his last shell, the more he saw the inadequacy of this unfamiliar gun with its short barrel and small bore. And somehow the front sight had been bent; and he was not an experienced pistol shot to begin with.

He set the gun to one side and cupped his hands about his mouth to form a megaphone.

"WALKER!" he shouted out into space. "Walker, can you hear me?"

There was a minute's silence before he got his answer. "I hear you, Brand."

The voice came from a point so much nearer to the ledge that the scarfaced man appeared to be talking conversationally. David fought back a panicky desire to hunch to the edge so he could look down and reassure himself they were farther away than the voice indicated. And he knew he would be performing an act of suicide if he allowed his head to show.

Lowering his tone to match Walker's, he called, "If I throw the film down, what guarantee do we get?"

The big man laughed. "Hell, man, we don't want you rollin' anymore rocks down at us. We just want to get that film and haul our asses out of these woods."

The way he said it sounded so temptingly simple.

"All right, Brand, I'm waiting." And his voice seemed closer still.

"Give me a minute. I've got to think about it."

"One minute."

"For Christ's sake, Walker!" David crabbed over to Starky and whispered, "Wait till you see them. Then shoot low. And shoot a lot."

Starky nodded vigorously while his shoulders hunched in a series of tension spasms.

"Brand, if you make us climb the rest of this fuckin' hill, we're damned well goin' to waste you— film or no film, and that's for fuckin' sure!" The voice was ominously close.

David scuttled his elbows back to the boulder, grabbed the Luger and hunched forward for a quick look.

Walker was moving upward, leaning into the steepness of the mountain, grabbing a manzanita bush with his left hand to pull himself along as his feet dug rungs in the steep earth. The others were spread out to either side of him, each keeping at least ten feet from his nearest companion in an irregular V formation like a migration of tired geese.

David whispered to Starky, "Not yet—not yet!"

Up and up they came, over the brow of the cliff where the mountain saucered before the ledge. They could move more easily now, but they were without protection from trees or the shield of the cliff. They moved forward with caution, rifles raised so the butts were just below their armpits. Walker, sweating profusely and grunting like a bear, was well ahead of the second man.

When the big man was less than ten yards from the twin muzzles of the machine gun, David grunted, "Now, Starky, now!"

Grabbing the protective branch, David leaned back and hauled it toward him, giving Starky a clear shot. The little man's hands immediately clenched tight on the triggers inset in the handles. Nothing happened.

"Now, Starky!" David cried. *"For God's sake, shoot!"*

"She won't—" Starky yelled, "she won't work!"

Tears of frustration welled to his eyes and he banged on the box that held the cartridge belt with his fist. "Work-Work-Work!"

Two of the riflemen snapped their guns to their shoulder and fired almost simultaneously. David heard the rip of a bullet tear through the leaves, and a ricochet from the rocks behind them.

Jumping up, he pointed his Luger at the rifleman now aiming at Starky and snapped away the final bullet. The shot missed, but kicked up dirt, causing the man to jump back clumsily, lose his balance and roll down the saucer toward the cliff.

And then suddenly the machine gun began to fire with an ear-shattering roar. It fired and kept on firing, jerking and ricocheting as it did. Starky clung fiercely to the punching handles that rattled his skinny frame so it appeared that the gun was in command of aiming and firing rather than the man.

The first bullets screamed out too high and they strafed the trees, cutting off branches and even slicing smaller tree trunks in half. Without stopping the fusilade, Starky managed to lower the barrels and rake a deadly stream of lead across the rocks where moments before the attackers had been standing, but after the first scream of surprise, the men had broken and run.

At the first burst of bullets, Walker's mouth jerked open as he bellowed in terror. He stumbled backward, rolled and began sliding down the hill. Scrambling to his feet with surprising agility, he half ran, half fell behind a tree, the path of the chattering machine gun's bullets kicking a crazy pattern in the dirt above, behind and on either side of him before gouging out a path across the trunk of the tree that protected him.

Starky sprayed the bullets across the area at random, the sound of the ricocheting bullets blending with the chattering noise of the gun and Starky's cries of exultation.

And then the gun choked and stopped firing as abruptly as it had begun.

"Jammed!" Starky cried, and began beating on the cartridge belt box with his fist. "She's jammed now for sure!"

Chapter Eleven

The jammed gun sat obstinately silent in the morning light. Threads of smoke still trailed from the twin muzzles and the barrels shimmered with heat from the firing.

His ears ringing, David felt pummeled in the sudden silence. For a second he stared uncomprehendingly at the valley spread out below him. Then he dragged the branch back so it again concealed Starky and the gun.

Starky scuttled into the cave and reappeared immediately with a rusty hammer and screwdriver. He attacked the problem with assurance, his skillful fingers moving knowingly about the machinery as David watched with increasing anxiety, frustrated by his own mechanical impotence.

"Shell's got jammed in her chamber," Starky grunted. "Not the right tools for it, but I'll get her."

The minutes stretched on until David found himself shaking with the tension of inactivity. Tapping Starky's shoulder, he gestured toward the rim before he crawled to the boulder and began to scan the mountainside below.

There was no sign of the men. Only the pockmarked earth, pitted boulders and torn trees bore evidence of the recent barrage. As he studied the terrain, David realized that Walker and his men had been so busy diving for cover they hadn't paused to look back and see Starky pounding on the disabled gun. As far as they knew, the firing had stopped as soon as they were no longer targets; it was logical for them to assume that the gun was again waiting in ambush until they next exposed themselves.

David tried to imagine what he'd do if he were pinned down in Walker's position, with what amounted to a machine-gun nest poised above him. For the first time in his life, David regretted that he'd been spared active combat and the training that went with it; he was just an amateur pitted against a ruthless man who was experienced in the business of killing other men.

But amateur or professional, the attackers had only a limited number of options. They could try climbing the cliff again, but so long as they believed the machine gun was operative it would seem a suicidal gesture. They could wait for reinforcements and split their attack—some pretending to climb the cliff to draw the fire while others crept up the trail to get an easy shot from the side while Starky's attention was focused down the mountain. Or they could try to find a way back around the ledge to climb above the cave to shoot down from above and behind the gun. David snapped his head about and scowled up at the steep slide and the area above the mouth of the cave: nothing appeared to have changed from yesterday; only a few wisps of high wind-driven clouds had begun to streak across the otherwise unbleached blue.

And the helicopter! The most logical move was to get that helicopter into action—it would provide a mobile platform for snipers while at the same time drawing the machine gun's fire away from any men that might be climbing the cliff or sneaking along the trail.

Why, David wondered, why in hell hadn't they brought the helicopter along in the first place? Could it have broken down, too? Maybe off on some other errand—perhaps bringing even more men? In any case, it would only be a matter of time before the machine was either repaired or returned.

His mind slipped feverishly from plan to counterplan. It was time to get out of this damned trap. Once he knew that they had to leave the security of the cave, options and combinations of options spun through his mind. Whatever he did, he couldn't simply solve the problem of one kind of attack—he had to be prepared to stop any combination Walker might throw at them. Their move was going to have to be one hell of a surprise.

Simultaneously, another detached part of his mind seemed to be running down its own checklist, reviewing the people and resources available to create this surprise: the gun, Starky, Maddy, Paige, himself. Rocks, boulders, the cave, picks, shovels, bailing wire, bullets, dynamite....

Dynamite! He could set sticks of dynamite around this shelf of rock in front of the cave—even booby-trap the machine gun by placing a stick in the ore cart directly under the weapon. He'd have to climb down the side of the mountain to a safe vantage point so that whenever the gang approached, he could plunge the exploder handle and blow out the whole side of the mountain. The initial explosion was sure to take out Walker and the men closest to him; the ensuing slide would crush stragglers below. He'd have to put a charge in the rocks above the ledge to dislodge any men that might have managed to climb over the cave.

But the helicopter was still a problem, and it was one he couldn't solve immediately: he'd have to face that situation if and when he got to it. At the very least, blowing the ledge in front of the cave would eliminate a place to unload gunmen from the air.

Scrambling back to Starky, now prying at the wedged shell with increasing frenzy, David hissed, "How's it coming?"

"She's gonna come. She's gonna let loose . . . any minute!"

"I'm going in to get some dynamite and set—"

Starky sank onto his heels, wiped a streak of grease across his sweaty forehead before he said with uncharacteristic gentleness, "Dynamite? Dynamite, Brandy? And what do you figure to do with that?"

"Blow hell out of them next time they come."

"Ain't gonna be no next time, Brandy. Soon's I get ol' Betsy going—"

"Starky, we haven't got time—"

The little man jerked back up onto his knees and began attacking the jammed shell with renewed fervor. "Don't need no time—no time a-tall. Just a couple minutes. I was just only startin' to catch the knack about the shootin' part." He beat the screwdriver furiously with the hammer.

Angrily, David spat, "Damn it, we need all the help we can get—"

"Got Betsy. Got m'knife. Don't need nothin' more."

David bit down on his lip; Starky was beginning to scrape ragged fingernails across the raw ends of his nerves. David stood quickly, ducked low and sprinted back to the cave. As he slipped through the curtains, he saw the lantern was lighted, but it took several seconds for his eyes to adjust to the surrounding gloom. Then he was able to make out Paige and Maddy sitting on the kegs near the dying embers of the fire.

Paige stood up cautiously. "David? David, for God's sake, what's happening out there?"

He regained his breath as he walked to her. "It's all right." Putting his arm across her shoulder, he hugged her to him in what he hoped was a reassuring gesture. "Gun just jammed. Starky's fixing it now."

"Christ, we thought you were all dead. This stinking place is nothing but one bloody echo chamber."

He grabbed the lantern off the barrel and walked back toward the storage area.

Setting the lamp on the floor, he knelt next to a crate on which the stenciled letters DYN----E were still faintly visible. He checked the cigar box with its tarnished blasting caps, each wrapped with twin wires. Touching the metal plunger on the exploder, he felt his way down to the two corroded terminals and then followed the wires to the big spool. They were the same wires and both unbroken.

"Maddy," he shouted, "give me a hand!" The instant the words rang out he realized what he'd done—here was something Paige could do, something that would make her feel needed and useful.

But, goddamnit, he needed something, too. He needed reliable assistance—without argument, without hysteria.

When Maddy appeared around the corner he handed her the heavy spool of wire; he picked up the exploder in one hand and the lantern in the other. Standing, he held the light above his head and turned to examine the contents of the cluttered area. Then he set the lantern on a crate and lifted a shovel that was propped in the corner.

To Maddy he said, "That's a spool of wire you've got. It's wired to an exploder I'm carrying—we'll have to stay close together. Don't stop suddenly. But if I stop, you stop, too. Okay?"

She nodded.

Hooking the little finger of the hand holding the shovel handle about the lantern's wire carrier, David picked up the light and made his way back to the fire area. Maddy walked silently by his side and a half a pace behind.

Paige was again seated on the keg, her hands clenched in her lap. David swallowed and nodded at her. "I'll be back in a couple of minutes. Then I'm going to need your help. You'll be all right?"

Her hands clenched and unclenched, but her voice was steady and flat. "I'll be all right. I'll be just fine."

"Come on, Maddy," David said, and walked to the mouth of the cave. There he set down the exploder, took the wire from Maddy and thrust the shovel handle through the hole in the wooden spool. Holding the handle in front of Maddy, he told her to reach out and take hold of the handle with one hand on either side of the spool. He pulled a length of the double wire from the coil, and the spool rolled irregularly but easily on its makeshift spindle.

After he'd described what he'd done, he said,

"Stay here behind the curtain and let it pay out as I pull. If it gets stuck or something, give it a quick pull so I'll know."

She nodded; David picked up the exploder and, holding the wires in his left hand so they wouldn't pull off the corroded terminals, he slipped through the curtains.

Once outside, he glanced down the mountain, across to Starky, still working on the gun, beyond the gun and concealing branch along the ledge to the head of the trail and finally up the mountain. There was no evidence that anything had changed except the sky. Heavy clouds had begun to spill over the crest, and white pennants strung across the sky above the valley created boats of deep shadows that sailed swiftly across the paler green of the sunlit meadows.

Crouching, David backed his way across the ledge, pulling the wires that writhed after him. When he got to the gun he ducked down next to Starky.

"How's it going?"

"Got her now," Starky grunted. "Dumb bastard dud shell never even went off. But I got her figured now. Won't be but a coupla minutes."

The irritation scorched David's stomach, touching off a fuse that flared through his veins and seared the inside of his skull. That goddamned idiot and his goddamned eternal coupla minutes! The world could blow up in his face and he'd still need a coupla minutes. David's hands involuntarily locked into fists and he hissed, "Goddamn it, we've got to get moving!"

Starky turned to look at him, then smiled with a kind of sweetness. Softly he said, "Brandy, you just worry too much, is all."

In that instant, David knew the little man was

mad, and abruptly he found himself laughing. It wasn't a funny laugh; it was harsh and irrational, but he couldn't stop.

Starky turned his attention back to the gun and said gently, "Just quit your frettin', Brandy. Betsy's 'most ready—then let them varmints come. Starky'll show 'em."

"You do that," David sighed, the tension dissipated with the laugh. "You do that, Starky. I'm going to lay some dynamite—make damned sure you don't shoot me."

Starky continued working on the gun with no indication he'd heard. David grabbed his shoulder, "Don't shoot me, you sonofabitch! I'm going to be right down there. So don't shoot!"

David gripped the wires again, picked up the exploder and made his way to where the edge dropped off less steeply. Setting the exploder on the trail, David got down on his hands and knees and crept forward till he could see the mountainside below; then he lay on his stomach and began studying the ground. There was no visible sign of Walker or any of the men. Next he examined the dished-out section immediately below him and tried to plot the course he'd have to take with the exploder that would get him back under the cave and protected from the slide when the dynamite blew.

Then he became aware of sounds of scuffling coming from the trail they had climbed the day before.

In one motion, he rolled onto his side, yanked the Luger from his pocket and sat up. Cocking the gun with his left hand, he thrust the gun forward and rested his elbows on his knees for support.

And at that moment the figure turned the last bend in the trail; David caught his chest in the notched rear sight, adjusted a fraction for the bent foreward post and snapped the trigger.

In the same instant he was aware the gun was empty, the last bullet wasted in the futile shot at Walker. The hammer fell on the firing pin with a barren click, and unaware, the man continued up the trail.

He was limping badly, his jaw contracted with the pain of every step, the tendons of his neck stood out like white ropes, his eyes were wide open and the color of spoiled oysters.

David shouted, "Hold it right there!"

But the man kept coming. He was tubercular thin with buck teeth.

David glanced behind him; he seemed to be alone. "I said *hold it!*"

The man stopped and stared. David recognized him as the first man that had tried to climb up the sandstone trough four days ago—the one he'd gotten with the rolling boulder.

Now the man was scrubbing the sleeve of his jacket across his eyes. Lowering his arm, he peered up the ledge at David. Then he cried, "Don't shoot! Oh-my-God, don't shoot!"

"Stay where you are!"

"I'm Reggie—they're going to kill me."

"I don't give a damn who you are."

"I'm Reggie. They took my guns away. They're going to kill me." He dropped to his knees and clasped his hands in prayer. "Dear God, mister, don't shoot. I'm just Reggie—Reggie Arnold."

And somehow in that moment as David stared down at him, the man dissolved and became a frightened kid. A kid who'd grown up in some city—slums, probably—played games and somehow managed to be accepted by the gang. And now he was trying to play by the gang's rules while inside he

was still a kid wanting to be accepted by somebody—begging to stay alive.

A shot rang out. A chunk of dirt exploded out of
the side of the mountain less than a yard from the
boy's head.

Shaking his clenched hands at David, Reggie
screamed, "Jesus, mister, Jesus!"

"All right. Grab the back of your neck with both
hands and come on." David had meant the
instructions to be calming with the proper amount
of authority; instead his voice sounded hoarse and
tough to his own ears.

Reggie's arms jerked upward and he looped them
over his head while struggling awkwardly to his feet.

Waving the pistol, David motioned him on up
the path. As he paused and then sidled by him,
David smelled the stench of both stale and fresh
sweat rising from damp stains. Reggie was wearing
a black leather jacket with the Rock Hounds
insignia emblazoned on the back. Around his waist
was a wide black leather belt set with sparkling
rhinestones and fastened with a buckle also
decorated with a Rock Hounds emblem.

As David bent over to pick up the exploder,
staccato bursts of machine-gun fire shattered the
air. The unexpected blasts staggered him and he fell
against the side of the mountain.

The firing stopped as abruptly as it had begun,
and Starky's face popped up from behind the brush
with a chimpanzee grin. "Got her now, Brandy!
Fixed her like new!"

His head ducked out of sight again as he proved
his words by spraying the bottom of the cliff where
the men had been, the spew of bullets ricocheting off
rocks with whining harmonics.

A second later Starky stopped firing and peered

around the side of the branch. "Brandy, watcha got
there?"

David prodded the man in the back with the
Luger. "His name is Reggie. They shot at him. He
says they're going to kill him."

"Shot at you, huh?" said Starky dryly. "Notice
they missed you."

Stepping out from behind the branch, Starky
appraised the Rock Hound with icy eyes. "Thought
they was fixin' to kill us. How come they want to kill
you?"

"'Cause I can't keep up—on account of my leg.
Walker kills any Rock that can't keep up; that's the
rules."

Magically the sliver of his knife appeared in
Starky's hand. He lowered his voice to just above a
whisper. "Boy, we got our own rules, too. We kill
any of you we catches—them's our rules."

The boy's eyes were riveted on the blade as he
shrieked, "Look at my leg! For Christsakes, look
here—here, I can't keep up no more!"

He tugged at a soiled trouser leg to reveal a
swollen ankle empurpled and caked with grime.
"Christ, I can't hardly stand no more."

"You got up that hill smart enough," Starky said,
flicking his thumb toward the trail.

David said, "Starky, this is the one I rolled the
rock on. Caught his leg."

Easing closer to the frightened youth, Starky
said, "Shoulda caught his head, Brandy."

David let go of the exploder and moved between
Starky and the boy. "You can't just kill him! You
can't murder a man in cold blood."

A rock shattered on the cliff above them; the
report of the rifle reached them an instant later. The
three men dropped to the ground behind the

branch, Starky swiveling to grasp the handles of the machine gun.

David tapped Starky on the shoulder and pointed toweard the trail where it turned onto the nearly level ledge. "They shot at him from down there; they've come up the trail."

"Not that one." Starky shook his head. "That one come from a ways off, else we wouldn't of heard it so long after the bullet hit. Just 'nother of them tricks—like him."

"I ain't no trick." Reggie spoke with more assurance now that Starky's back was turned to him while the gun was being attended. "Ain't no more trick than Warren."

Starky said nothing. David asked, "Who's Warren?"

"Warren's dead. He's shot and dead just for killing a lousy buzzard."

David remembered the scene all too vividly. "Why'd Walker kill him for that?"

"We only get paid for killing them big bastards— condors. Walker don't want no other animals lying around dead or somebody might ask questions."

"Who's paying you?" David asked quickly.

"Fucked if I know."

David punched the Luger against his chest. "Who's paying?"

"God, mister—I don't know." The whine was back in his voice. "Walker and Collins—they do all the talkin'. We're just along for the loot. Some of the old Rocks say there's got to be one big mother laying out that kind of heavy bread for wasting a bunch of dumb birds. Me, I don't know and I don't give a shit."

Starky turned from the gun and faced them, saying, "They're laying back, Brandy—waitin'. And if I was us, I'd be mighty hot to figure just what they was waitin' on." He smiled brightly at David; it was a smile that demanded a question.

"And what are they waiting for?"

"They's waiting on the trick to go off. An' him there is the one who's supposed to make the trick."

"But what the hell *is* the trick?"

"Brandy, it don't matter—if we just cut his throat, he ain't goin' to make no tricks on us." In one effortlessly fluid motion, Starky was on his feet, crouched like a wrestler, the blade glinting in his hand.

David jumped up. "Starky, goddamn it, no! Maybe they killed Blinky—maybe they killed a lot of other people. But this kid hasn't killed anybody— not that we know of. If we wipe him out just because he's part of the gang, we're not one bit better than they are."

Now the little man turned on David, the knife flicking back and forth like the head of a nervous rattler. "Brandy, Starky never figured he was better than nobody. And he ain't no worse, neither—he just figures to stay alive."

"All right—all right! We're all going to stay alive." David swung around to face Reggie, "Okay, kid, either you're going to help us or I'll turn you over to Starky."

"Christ, mister," he croaked, "anything you say. Anything—but Jesus, don't let him at me." Unconsciously he clutched his throat with both hands as he pleaded.

"So tell us—how many are there? Where are they? What are they doing and what do they plan to do?"

Reggie's mouth opened and closed twice before he could make his words come out. "There are two—two down there." He pointed down the cliff toward where the first attack had begun. "And two—maybe more—come up the trail after me." He pointed to the head of the trail, nodding to affirm his own words. "Then Walker was going to join up with Sam and Webber up there—" He pointed up the mountain above the cave. Cocking his head, he squinted upward.

He stepped sideways and raised his left hand to shield his eyes from the light that bounced off the cliff above the cave. "They circled the trail so they could get above you and shoot down at your back." He took another step, still scanning the hill.

David moved around him, searching the area near the posts that held the cable from which the carrier hung suspended. For an instant he thought he saw a movement behind a huge rock, but the shadows from the scudding clouds gave deceptive motion to all the mountain. He called Starky to him. "Hey, take a look up there."

A second later he sensed the boy's absence. Whipping his head around, he was just in time to see Reggie finishing his sprint to the machine gun, moving like a weasel, fast and with no sign of a limp.

David managed a strangled shout before he hurled himself after the leather-clad figure; Starky was behind David as he raced toward the gun. But Reggie had kicked the two stones out from under the wheels of the ore cart, shoved the branch aside and was leaning all his weight against the vehicle, which had already begun rolling down the decline. And as the cart picked up momentum, Reggie's legs churned faster, pounding his feet against the ledge.

David dived at the jacketed waist in an attempt to stop the cart and give Starky a chance to block the wheels again. But his tackle fell short and he could only wrap his arms about the pumping knees, jerking Reggie's feet out from under him.

Then Reggie's grip tore loose from the cart and

his hands slid down the side until the coupling hook slammed him between the legs and continued traveling up his trousers where it caught under the wide, rhinestone-encrusted belt.

David clung to Reggie's knees, spreading his legs and dragging the sides of his shoes along the rock to give better purchase, but the heavily loaded ore cart continued rattling down the shelf toward the edge, dragging the two men with it.

Reggie began clutching at his waist, trying to press the hook out from under his belt. Starky flung himself on David's ankles and reared back only to have his heels dragged across the ground.

The runaway cart had just begun to slow from their combined weight when the front wheels dipped across the ledge, the back end levered upward and the cart catapulted over the edge.

Reggie's heels snapped up and slammed David under the ribs, knocking the wind out of him and breaking his tackle.

The back end of the cart continued rising as the front dropped off the precipice, and Reggie was lifted high in a great arc, suddenly screaming in an unearthly sound as he was yanked upward like the tail of a kite.

The cart and the weapon and the man finally crashed to the side of the mountain, where they bounced and continued to roll through the heavy brush. Sounds of the cart's progress carried up to the ledge long after Reggie's screams had stopped and the vehicle had disappeared.

Starky slid off David's legs and peered into his friend's eyes. The old man's face was the color and texture of a walnut except where tears had washed the dust away; now more tears ran across to his nose and down the crow's feet at the corner of his other eye.

"Gone," he cried softly. "Betsy's gone. Brandy, whyn't ya let me kill the sumabitch? Why, Brandy?" His sobs were wrenched from deep inside his chest, choking off his words so they became unintelliglble grunts of pain.

David couldn't bear to watch the man's face; pressing the palms of his hands against the stone, he pushed himself to a sitting position. Starky swung himself around to sit in front of him.

"Brandy, I coulda kilt him. We coulda had Betsy. We coulda had a chance."

There were no words; Starky had been so right and he had been so wrong—suicidally wrong. But he had to say something—some words, no matter how meaningless, such as one says at the funeral of a distant relative. He tried to apologize and mumbled something about killing a man in cold blood, of assuming the role of judge, jury and executioner.

Starky squirmed and shook his head. "Brandy, you wasn't to kill him, *I* was to kill him. And we ain't got judges and juries. And there ain't no need—no more than if a bear come after you or a rattler climbs under your tarp. You don't need no judge nor jury— you just kill him. You don't mean him no harm, Brandy—you just kill him afore he kills you."

David nodded. In that moment he could feel the logic of Starky's words. Because he had spent so much of his adult life in remote parts of the world, he had come to think of himself as a man at home in primitive wilderness. In this second he recognized that he had no more become a part of the wilderness than a Boy Scout on a camping trip. He had merely carried civilization with him like a backpack and carried the same concepts out again.

This time the shot hit the outer side of the ledge, blowing a chunk out of the rock. Fragments flew across the ledge like a wild charge of grapeshot and rattled against the stone slide behind them. The report boomed up from far down the mountain. Another shot rang out from the end of the trail.

Starky flipped himself away from the edge and onto his belly.

David rolled against the rock as another shot hit the slide and whined away.

"They're gonna come," Starky said. "They gonna try shootin' first, but they're gonna come swarming like buzzards to a carcass."

David's eyes flicked across the ledge—to the impotent Luger where he'd dropped it in his dash toward Reggie.

The exploder! It was too late to blow the slide— but they could still close the mouth to the cave.

Starky jabbed a finger toward David's arm and said, "Brandy, you're bleedin' like a stuck sow."

David glanced at his shoulder and then down at his upper arm; as he watched, blood began to slide down the inside of his wrist below his cuff and spilled down his palm. In an abstracted way he watched his own blood flow and nodded at Starky. He was, indeed, bleeding like a stuck sow.

"Grab the gun," David said. He crawled to the exploder, leaving a trail of bloody palmprints on the rock. He picked up the exploder and, doubled low in order to present the smallest possible target, dashed to the cave. Starky waited until he was past and followed behind him.

Without a shot having been fired, they reached the curtain and hurtled into the cave.

Maddy screamed: "David? David, is it you? Pa?"

"David, thank God," Paige said. "We didn't know what was happening. All that shooting—and you're bleeding."

Shouting above her words, David bellowed, "Paige! Come up here and watch!"

Maddy moved forward. "I couldn't hold the wire any longer, so I set it down—"

To Paige, David said, "Stay back of the curtain, but let us know soon's you see anything. Anything at all!"

Spinning on his heel, he began reefing in the wires beneath the burlap.

As he bent over he suddenly felt weak.

Flames flashed behind his eyes and he was barely aware of trying to straighten up before he lost his balance and was swallowed into a blackness beyond space.

Chapter Twelve

When he regained consciousness, his sleeve had been trimmed off and his arm was bandaged above the elbow. His head rested in Maddy's lap and she held a cup of water to his lips.

"Drink," she said.

"Gotta get—" he began groggily.

He clenched his teeth and twisted his mouth away from the cup. He was aware of the vaulted roof of the cave, the blotches of light straining through the canvas. He made out Paige's silhouette against the curtain, a stripe of light cutting down the center of her face. Starky came to bend over him, peering anxiously into his eyes.

As he struggled off Maddy's lap and raised himself on his elbows, then onto the palms of his hands, David asked, "How long?"

Starky shook his head. "Couple—few minutes, mebbe."

David raised his voice. "Paige, they doing anything out there?"

The curtain moved slightly, widening the streak on Paige's face; after a second she said, "Nothing. I haven't seen anything at all."

David got to his feet shakily.

Pointing to the bandage, he said, "Thanks for the patch. How bad is it?"

He suspected it was bad enough; his whole arm had begun to throb from the effort it had taken to bring himself upright. The rest of the aches seemed minor.

"Not so much deep, Brandy. But she's a wide one and crooked. Most likely a piece of stone caught it."

David nodded. "Let's get the dynamite set up; they'll be coming any minute."

"What dynamite, Brandy? They ain't no dynamite."

"The dynamite! In the box back there—I saw it."

David walked stiffly toward the storage area.

Kneeling in front of the box with the stenciled DYN----E, he lifted off the box containing the blasting caps and set it on the ground as gently as he could. They were the tricky part. He'd once seen a wrangler lose an eye and part of a hand when he mishandled a blasting cap back on the ranch in Montana.

David pulled the broken Swiss army knife from his pocket and pried open the lid of the dynamite box. It was empty except for the bottom layer; there were three sticks. One was half disintegrated; the second crumpled like ashes the moment David tried to lift it. The third stick held firm.

David turned to face Starky. "Where's the rest of it?"

"There wasn't no more. Them miners didn't leave hardly nothing at all."

"For Christ's sake, man, we can't blow the cave with only one stick!"

Starky leaped backward and pointed an accusative finger toward David, jabbing it back and forth like a child shooting a make-believe gun. "Brandy, we ain't blowing this cave!" he gasped. "This here's Starky's cave and it's not gonna get blown!"

"We've got to, you idiot!"

With a leap, Starky landed in front of David, grabbed his shirt front with his left fist and flashed the knifeblade in his right. "This-here cave doesn't get blowed up!"

Calmly as he could, David replied, "All right, Starky—fine. We'll save the cave. Maddy will die. Paige will die. You and I'll die—but we'll save your goddamn cave."

The little man hunkered back on his heels; his eyes were unfocused. "Brandy—Maddy's gonna die?"

"If you'd rather have the cave, Walker's going to kill Maddy. Going to kill her along with the rest of us."

Starky loosened his grip on David's shirtfront. "Brandy, you're sure?"

"I've never been more sure."

The little man thought for a long moment: his eyes shifted restlessly and the tautness along his jaw eased. Finally he sighed and said, "Hell, Brandy—it's nothing but an ole Chumash Indian cave nohow."

David nodded sympathetically. "I'll take the dynamite halfway up the side and pack it. With luck, it'll drop the near side of the slide right over this end of the cliff and block the mouth of the cave."

Starky shook his head. "Ain't gonna work, Brandy. One charge ain't gonna blow that slide and get all them rocks rollin'. Need mebbe a half dozen—prob'ly more."

Starky rubbed the back of his hand across his nose as he pondered. Then he pointed to the ceiling. David turned and saw a dot of daylight filtering in through the pipe, spotlighting the circle of stones that formed the fireplace.

"Supposin' I was to blow the slide so's to keep them piss-ants from gettin' to Maddy—from gettin' to us—I'd blow the sumabitch?"

David looked at Starky and back at the ceiling again. He heard the words without being able to sense any information from them. But he now accepted Starky's intuitive grasp of the primitive rules by which they were fighting.

"Okay," David said. "You'd blow the slide without blowing the slide—is that what you're saying?"

Starky nodded. "I'd feed them wires down through that there smoke vent and pack the stick hard in the side of the cave." He pointed toward the inside arch near the entrance. "Once that wall blows, all them stones restin' on this side of the cliff's goin' to go. And once they get a-rollin', nothin's goin' to stop the rest from followin' after."

Starky got to his feet and started toward the mouth of the cave.

David pushed himself up and followed; Starky grabbed the spool of wire from the floor of the cave where Maddy had set it and scuttled past Paige and through the curtain.

Paige shook her head wearily. "No sound."

"There will be," David said. "Lot of sound."

He bent down and picked up the wires, then he pulled back the curtain so he could watch Starky's progress. The little man was already fifteen feet straight up the slide, backing up, his legs pumping like pistons, the shovel held waist-high with the wire unreeling behind him.

All the while, David was aware of the strain in his ears as he anticipated the barrage of shots that was sure to come. In his mind's eye he saw carnations of blood spurt across the man's chest; saw him collapse back onto the stones and topple down the rocky pile.

Miraculously, there were no shots. Starky made it over the crest near the post with the loading platform swaying on its cable.

But even after Starky had disappeared, the tug on the wires continued. David hadn't imagined the cave to be so deep as to demand all that wire. Finally the tugging stopped.

David handed the wires to Paige and ran back into the cave, where he peered at the circle of light. Seconds passed, then minutes. Finally the wires protruded down from the pipe.

Jumping, David caught one wire, then the other, and pulled hard until he had a dozen feet of free wire. He wrapped a loop around a stalactite formation, then over to another, and finally to the wall of the cave.

There was a deep crack halfway down the wall that was only slightly longer and wider than the stick of dynamite. He hurried to the box and lifted out the one intact stick and set it gently on the ground. From the cigar box he took out one of the blasting caps and unwrapped the two wires that stuck out from one end. Holding the dynamite in his left hand toward the lantern's light, he inserted the cap, doing it as gingerly as though pushing his thumb down on a hypodermic needle.

David carried the prepared stick to the hole and

slid both the cap and stick as far into the niche as they would go. Then he twisted the two slender wires onto the larger insulated ones. He crammed the excess wire into the hole, picked up a handful of sand and gravel and, forming a V with his two palms, funneled it into the remaining space. With his fingers, he cautiously packed the sand and gravel against the wires, cap and dynamite stick. Then he crawled about the floor until he found more rocks and put them in behind the sand and gravel.

Now, unless the dynamite was too old or the blasting cap was too corroded, the bomb was ready.

He set the lantern on the barrel at the far side of the cave to obscure the wires running from the smoke vent, across the ceiling and down to the dynamite hole.

Maddy remained seated on the barrel near the dying embers.

"Come with me."

She followed him, stopping when he bent over to pick up the exploder, then moving forward again as he passed through the curtain.

Outside the cave, Paige said, "They haven't shown yet. Nothing at all. Christ, I almost wish they'd do something. Anything!"

"We're going to blow up the cave. Stay close to me. And stay low."

He took a look up the slide. There was no sign of activity—neither of Starky, nor of Walker and his men. Thirty feet down the trail was a boulder big enough to protect them from any possible flash-back. Crouching, with the exploder tucked against his chest, David backed his shoulders against the upside of the cliff, grabbed Maddy's hand and whispered back at Paige—"Low and inside."

Then, hurrying forward, David let the wires play out behind him so they ran diagonally across the slide toward the top of the cliff, bending among the rocks. But he kept a secure grip with his other hand at the terminals to keep the connections from ripping loose. They skirted the ledge where the machine gun had been, behind the branch, along the side of the trail to the boulder. The width of the trail hid them from being seen from below; the bend along the mountain covered them from the far end, but their rush past the base of the slide seemed to last an eternity—perhaps a minute.

The women crouched behind the boulder; David set the exploder beside them. Then he looked up the mountainside toward the platform and Starky, but the cliff blocked his view of the upper landing. He could only see the sky above—and that had become ominously dark. Storm clouds drove low across the peaks and there was a distant rumble of thunder. Overhead were cumulus clouds following anvil-topped thunderheads.

David eased out from the edge and stole his way back toward the cave; he knew he had to be exposing himself to possible shots from below, but it was the only way he could see the butte over which Starky had disappeared. Where the hell had he gone—he couldn't blow the cave with the sonofa-bitch standing over the blast.

Then he saw the little man pumping his arms against the thunderheads. He was above the cave mouth, way up on the four-by-three foot platform that swayed from its cable. Now he crouched between the two rusty wheels that hooked the platform to the cable. Hopping like a demented gibbon, he semaphored his arms wildly to catch David's attention.

The instant David waved back, Starky jabbed both hands off to his left—palms upright, thumbs cocked. David spun and looked down the trail—

there was no one in sight. He glanced back at Starky, who was shaking his head violently and jabbing his hands closer to the cave and the rock ledge. Then Starky held up his right hand and extended two fingers separated in a wide V. Two. Two had made it up the cliff beneath the impossible, goat-defying cave! Then where were the others?

Crouched, David ran back to the boulder. "Maddy," he whispered, "grab this handle here"— he guided her hand down to the T-bar on the exploder—"and when I say *now*, push down as hard as you can."

"Always Maddy!" Paige snapped. "I'm not a paraplegic, you know! I can damned well do something!"

"All right, Paige—you do it," he said. "Do it hard—sharp—in one quick shove."

Maddy sank against the cliff and Paige took her place, crouching above the exploder. David crawled away from the protective boulder to where he could see the mouth of the cave and most of the flat shelf; the branch blocked the rest.

And he waited. It seemed a long time; rain began to fall and spattered on his back.

Then a head appeared at the end of the shelf. It was a head with a wool hat on it. Next David saw a forearm, then another hand clutching a pistol. The man hauled himself up onto the shelf and flopped over. For a moment he sat there panting, his inquiring gun moving uncertainly back and forth examining the cliff. Satisfied, he heaved himself to his feet. He was a big man with a leather jacket decorated with the insignia of the Rock Hounds. He wore motorcycle boots.

Seconds later another man clambered onto the shelf. He also wore a leather jacket and heavy boots, but he was hatless with shoulder-length blond hair.

The two men stood slightly apart, studying the cliff, the slide and the hill above it. Then the blond man noticed the camouflaged curtain wave in the rising wind. Signaling with his pistol, he began approaching the mouth of the cave; the man with the hat sidled past him to approach from the far side.

The big man stopped and grunted "George, you go on in—I'll cover."

"Not me. I'm not going in there."

The first gestured angrily with his pistol, "George, I said to get your ass in gear!"

"You first, shithead!" the blond man spat. "I'm not gettin' my nose shot off for nobody."

"Christ, they're hell an' gone over the ridge by now."

"Okay—you're so sure, you stick your face in there."

The big man hesitated. "Maybe we ought to wait for Walker and Bunko."

David felt the words in his skin: where the hell *were* Walker and the other man coming from? Up the trail behind him—behind the girls and the exploder? Still on his belly, David inched awkwardly back to the boulder.

"Now?" Paige whispered. "Now, David?"

He shook his head. "I'll tell you when."

A wilder spattering of rain blew across them, sounds of the impending storm rippled through the mountain forests. David raised his head again and looked around the boulder. The man called George had disappeared; only the canvas curtain undulated in the rising winds. Then he saw the other man follow him into the cave.

"Now, Paige, now!" he yelled.

And he looked back and saw Paige standing above the exploder, the handle shoved full down, and nothing had happened.

God, David thought as he ran back and shoved the girl aside, jerking the exploder from her, the dynamite's too old. Dead. Won't ignite.

But as he looked down at the box he saw that one wire had pulled off its terminal. He grabbed the loose wire and jammed it against the terminal as he drew the plunger up and slammed the bar down as hard as he could.

Chapter Thirteen

David felt the explosion before he heard it. A quiver of the earth, an electric *thrummmm*, then a spasm in the butte above the cave; a fiery bellow billowed the canvas curtain up and tore it from its fastenings. There was a blast of yellow-black air, a rumble of discontent from the rocks above—nothing more. The slide did not give. But God, the ancient dynamite had done its job.

The three of them went up the trail and crossed the ledge toward the now gaping blackened mouth of the cave.

When they reached the canvas panels lying on the stone, David guided the women to the inside edge of the ledge.

He slid into the cave with his back against the wall, straining his eyes to pierce every shadow. He couldn't shrug off the foreboding that all their luck was within seconds of running out. He half expected the men to be standing there facing him with drawn guns, and the shots to flash out without warning.

It took willpower to move one foot forward, then the next. Nobody appeared; no shots exploded.

The cave was lighter than it had been. The blast had blown out a portion of the ceiling, and a large section of the side wall had crumbled onto the floor. Even as he watched, other stones and rocks clattered down from above. The cooking area and the kerosene fire had been blown out, leaving only rubble and blackened walls. The bitter smell of dynamite filled the cavern. He spotted a shoeless foot under a pile of boulders, and then, ten feet away, he saw the other man's body partly covered by rocks and lit eerily by the shaft of light from a hole above.

It was tomblike. He turned and stumbled back out to the mouth of the cave and over to the women.

"We did it!" he blew out a tired sigh. "They're both gone. Now there's only Walker and one other. And I'll bet that—"

"David!" Paige gasped.

The gun was jabbed against his lower back with such force that for an instant he thought he'd been hit by a bullet.

"You bet wrong," a man rasped. It was the granite-cold voice of Walker.

But the voice came from somewhere else. Very slowly, David began to twist his head. He caught a glimpse of Walker peering up over the corner of the ledge, his bone-bald head with its jagged scar glistening in the rain. His elbows rested on the rock, the pistol pointed up at David. But it was the other one, a red-bearded man, who held the barrel of an automatic shotgun against David's tailbone.

Walker grunted. "If they move, Bunko, shoot 'em." Disdainfully Walker chucked the pistol so it landed almost at David's feet. Then somehow he found a foothold in the cliff, clutched at the ledge with the hand in the cast and heaved his bulk onto the shelf. Gasping, he lurched forward to pick up the pistol and straightened to face David and the women.

For a moment he stood swaying and wiping the rain from his eyes.

There was a nearby flash of lightning and then a roll of thunder.

"All right, you sonofabitch," he spat. "For openers, the film."

David raised his hand to his right pants pocket and brought it out empty. Then he put his other hand in his left pocket, fighting for time. The rain increased, and for a moment slashed furiously across the ledge.

David shook his head.

"Must have dropped it," he said finally.

"You're cute, Brand—very cute," Walker said, his voice softened by the rain. "But you know the score. You lost. Nothing personal, but you're dead."

"I'm dead—" David repeated, still futilely patting his pockets.

"Just give us the film," Walker nodded reassuringly, "and we kill you quick and easy."

Paige laughed suddenly. "So you're going to kill us quick and easy. Just like that!"

Walker scarcely bothered to look at her. "There are other ways, baby. Lots of other ways."

There was something insane about it all. David felt that if he could only catch hold of a bit of sanity, everything would fall into perspective.

With all the authority he could manage, he said, "Now, damn it, Walker, let's be sensible. You can't just kill us here and forget about it. To begin with, we're fairly well known people. Miss Evans is the publisher of *The Explorer* magazine and I've got something of a name myself."

Walker grinned. "Hell, why didn't ya say so, Brand? Why, shit, I suppose I should want to shake your hand or something."

The man called Bunko laughed.

"If we don't return," said David, "there'll be a search for us you can't believe. And they'll find us and—"

Walker grinned more genuinely. "Now I'd like to see that, Mr. Brand. There've been people lost in here before—pretty important people, too. Big military brass and like that. And you know what, Mr. Brand? Never did find hide nor hair, never found so much as a button."

"They're probably looking for us right now," said Paige. "And they'll get you! Will they ever get you!"

Bunko jabbed his shotgun against Paige's breast.

"She's the one that done it, Walker," Bunko said. "I saw her push the plunger."

"Oh, she did?" Walker turned toward Paige. "You killed two of the finest boys I had working for me since the Seebees?"

"Fine boys!" Paige spat. "Murderers!"

"Ooh, lady—" Walker spoke the words softly and shook his head slightly, but the sound was more menacing than if he'd bellowed. "Ooh, lady, are you screwed up. We're not the murderers—you and do-gooders like you are the murderers. But we're big, bigger'n General Motors, and we're here to look out for the American people instead of some god-damned condors."

Paige gasped again. "Tell your goon to stop jabbing me with that gun!" Her voice, though breathless, was steely. "Goon!"

Bunko jabbed her with the shotgun again, then turned and jabbed Maddy.

"Cut it out!" said David.

But the bearded man did it again and Walker laughed.

"Stop—please—stop!" Maddy cried, groping toward the barrel. She caught it with one hand, then the other, and twisted it away from her body. He jabbed it back at her and with an angry cry she yanked it violently. The gun seesawed for a moment and then the girl stumbled back just as the gun went off.

In one dreadful flash David saw the look on the girl's face, more of surprise than pain, the corners of her mouth drawn down with the suddenness of it. As her body jackknifed from the blast, slamming her back against the rock, he saw the blouse ripped open to expose flesh torn apart by the pellets and a gaping blue-red crater that instantly filled crimson.

He watched in horror as her body crashed face down on the rocks at the base of the slide. One arm quivered, spasmed out straight, and then she was still.

"Bastards!" David yelled.

Walker's back was slightly turned as he looked down at Maddy, and David flung himself onto the huge man's shoulders, locking one arm around his neck and grabbing for the hand that held the pistol. But Walker slammed his elbow into David's ribs, then whirled and delivered a backhand blow to the side of David's head that sent him to the ground. Simultaneously, David saw the bearded man knock Paige down with a swing of the shotgun stock.

The rain washed across David's face; tiny streams began spilling through the rock slide and running onto the ledge where Maddy lay.

Walker turned and raised his pistol to point it

down at David. But David's attention was attracted
past the man to a motion above him on the hill. At
first it appeared to be some kind of a flying object;
then it became a platform, the old one hanging from
the cable. It was coming down at them, no more
than ten feet above the ground. Then he saw
Starky—his face contorted crouching on the planks
of the platform, hanging on to one of the braces with
his left hand while holding a noose in his other—a
kind of lariat made of doubled-up wire.

Walker saw David ignoring his pistol and staring
up the hill and he heard the sound of the rusty
wheels spinning on the cable. And at the same time
he heard the cry of a cougar coming from the
platform.

Whirling, Walker glanced up and reflexively
fired at the platform. But he was too late—the noose
whipped down around Bunko's neck and as the
platform screamed past, the slack came out of the
wire and the red-bearded man was yanked upward
and across the ledge. He struck out wildly, clawing
at his neck, but the force jerked him off the shelf like
an opening parachute snatching a man out of a
plane.

Walker ran across the ledge, firing at Starky.
David scrambled to his feet, charged at Walker and
threw a diving block behind the man's knees. The
momentum was enough to propel the body over the
cliff. With a high cry Walker dropped out into space
and disappeared from David's view.

The platform with Starky aboard was still
hurtling down the mountainside, the body of the
bearded man dangling like a marionette from the
wire.

David staggered to the edge and looked over,
half expecting Walker to be getting to his feet

unscathed. But no—the man's bulk lay at the bottom; it had fallen face down on one of the small trees cut in two by the machine gun's bullets and had been impaled on the sharp stump.

A rock clattered down the slide and rolled across the ledge toward David; more rocks rumbled uneasily above him.

David ran across the ledge to Paige and pulled her to her feet. Above them rocks were beginning to come down in flurries now. In seconds the entire side of the mountain was going to let go.

Slinging Paige's arm across his shoulder, David half pulled, half carried her through the mouth of the cave and on past the blown-out fireplace area and beyond where the machine gun had first been.

And with each step, the rumble of the slide became louder until the cave walls trembled. The sand and smaller stones spattered from the roof and walls of the cave. The avalanche kept building a thunderous booming bellow; the wall, already weakened by dynamite, buckled, sending rocks and boulders into the cave. Rocks cascaded, filling to the roof the hollows where they had slept. Only then, the rush of sound diminished like the roar of a train being sucked into the night. The rain waters had completed the job the explosive had begun; the cave was totally blocked, totally dark.

David hugged Paige close, sheltering her with his arms and legs as he kept himself pressed against the wall. They stayed like that for long minutes after the roar was gone; occasionally a rock would roll across the cave floor toward them.

Finally she said, "Is it over?"

"It's over," David said flatly. There was no room for another rock to come in; there was no room for anyone to get out.

"They killed Maddy!" Paige whispered.

David answered through clenched teeth, "Yes—they killed her."

Paige sucked a half-sob, "She was so—so brave..."

"Yes," David said. He fought to keep his emotions in check. She was indeed brave—and a lot more. "And her father saved our lives."

Even as he spoke the words he realized the irony of it. Saved them for what? To be buried alive? It was impossible to conceive that they could dig their way through the tons of fallen rock. The tools were buried from them, too; even with powerful hoists and lifts it would take a team of professionals a week or more to dig them out. They would have to go out the back way—if Maddy had been right, and there was a back way. She'd said it was dangerous, but it was better than just sitting here waiting to die.

"We'll follow the rails," he said, reaching for Paige's hand in the dark and starting for the back of the cave. The underground river—the river he'd heard before—could lead them out.

It was not easy going. The declines became more abrupt. He'd had a lantern when he'd explored it before. Again and again they came to divisions. If only Maddy were here to guide them in the dark—oh, dear God—Maddy. Sometimes David thought he heard the rush of water off to the left, sometimes to the right. Always they seemed to be bearing toward their left; always they went deeper into the heart of the mountain. The water was the key—the water must flow out someplace. "Got to get to the underground river!"

Now he was walking on the wooden cross ties—it was easier than straddling the rails. Suddenly his foot came down on a tie under which the earth had been eroded. The rotted timber gave way and his leg plunged through the gap; his body twisted as he fell. He heard himself yell with the pain as his knee snapped; an icepick of shock spiked through the cartilage between the two leg bones.

"David?" Paige's voice came out of the dark. "David?"

He pulled himself up from the hole; sitting, he rocked back and forth squeezing his knee. "My knee," he gasped. He felt as if he'd been slammed in the stomach, and there was nothing left in his lungs.

"Can you walk?"

He pushed himself up on his one leg. When his other foot touched the ground, a moan escaped from him into the darkness of the cave, where it trailed off in ghostly echoes.

"Can you walk if you lean on me?"

He ran his hand up over her back and across to her shoulder. They moved on, but slowly, every step fiery agony for him. The shaft was treacherously steep at times now.

"I hear the water!" she said suddenly. "Wait here." And she was gone.

He called to her but there was no answer. Bracing one hand against the wall, he ducked his head and started after her. Then he had to bend at the waist; finally he could go no further without bending his knee, so he sat down. The rush of water could be heard clearly.

Then he felt Paige's hands touching him.

"This tunnel goes down to the water," she panted. "But it's very steep. Gets steeper and narrower all the time. I stopped when I couldn't keep from sliding all the way."

"I'll give it a try."

"David, no! I'm going first!"

He started to object.

"I'll go first," she repeated.

It occurred to him then that the slide might become very narrow before it reached the water. Narrow enough to wedge him fast, but perhaps still wide enough to allow her slender body to slide through. The odds for her were best if she went ahead of him.

"Okay," he said, "you go first."

They started like that, David hunching up on the palms of his hands and shoving himself forward onto his hips. It was too much work for little ground gained, so he swung himself around and with the help of his good leg managed to drag himself backward more successfully. As the tunnel dropped off ever more sharply, he was able to move even faster; it was slickly damp now and the rush of water seemed very close below them.

Paige called, "David, I'm going to slide now."

"I'll be behind you."

"Oh, God—"

It was a long, clear cry that floated up the stone tube till it stopped abruptly.

David tried to hear if there had been a splash, but he couldn't be sure. All he heard was the heavy stir and push of the underground stream. Then he struggled to turn himself around, but the tunnel had become so narrow it was impossible. He would have to hunch back up to where it was wide enough before he could manage to slide down feet first. He doubted he had the strength.

He humped backward until he felt himself beginning to slide. Then he lay back, clasped his hands over his head and gave one last push with his foot.

It was enough. He picked up speed at a dizzying rate. The sides scraped his shoulders and elbows and he imagined falling in shallow water or onto a rock.

And he shot out of the tunnel, fell twenty feet and plunged into icy water.

Immediately he began flailing his arms, trying to fight to the surface without being certain whether he was headed up or down.

He broke the surface, gasping. He kept his head above water with a little paddling motion: there was light! It was dim—a dark purplish-blue—but it was definitely not tomb black. They were in some sort of a giant grotto.

Then he realized the current was carrying him swiftly downstream; along the sides of the river he could make out irregular forms sliding smoothly behind him. The cold water numbed him and took the pain from his leg and shoulder.

"Paige!" he shouted.

"I'm here, David." Her voice came from the riverbank nearby. Then, dimly, he saw her. She was standing at the edge, waving frantically; he was already being carried past her. He tried to turn and swim upstream but the pull of the river was too powerful.

"I'm already past you."

"Keep going," she called.

The river rounded a slight bend and it became lighter; another bend and there was a horizontal band of daylight. David was sucked toward the band, which appeared steadily wider as he approached.

Then the ledge of rock slid above him and the river pushed him out of the mountain out into the daylight and the pelting rain, into the river that flowed along the meadows of Starky's Valley.

He swam to the shallows near the bank.

Paige appeared minutes after him. Half swimming, half wading, he anticipated her, pulled her to the side of the river and boosted her onto the bank.

"Oh, Lord, David—" she breathed as she pushed at her wet hair.

The rain continued beating down on them, but it seemed a merciful rain and they lay luxuriating in the miracle of being alive.

Then they heard the *whap-whap-whap* of the helicopter—now loud, now soft—as it maneuvered above them along the mountain. David pushed himself to his feet and limped away from the river, trying to locate the aircraft. First he saw the gash of rocks and boulders left by the slide. Then he saw the helicopter where the ledge had been, swinging back over the dome above the cave. He shook his head and swore silently, "The bastards never quit."

He limped back to where Paige lay. "We've got to get back to Starky. I'd guess he'd go to the house."

"Who's to know?" she said in a good imitation of the little man's voice.

He reached down and pulled her up into his arms. He could feel her body through their wet clothes as though they were both naked.

"The plane," Paige said. "He'd be near the plane. Remember, he wants you to fly us out."

"Paige, I can't fly. I haven't flown for twenty years."

"Not since?"

"No."

"Can you run better than you can fly?"

He glanced down at his leg. "You've got a point."

Then he turned to look at Starky's house nearly a mile away and the stand of cotton woods around it. By stretching, he was able to see a bit of the yellow airplane.

"Let's go," he said.

But as he started across the field he stumbled and nearly fell. The cold of the river had numbed the pain of his knee, but the injury was still there. Looking down the riverbank, he saw some sticks washed up at the water's edge. He hobbled to a pile and searched until he found one with a forked branch at the end. By wedging it between two stones and leaning on it he managed to break it until it was approximately the length he needed. With the forked end under his armpit it served as a passable crutch, and they started off across the meadow.

Halfway through the field, David glanced back to where the helicopter had been. The pilot had evidently given up trying to land and was hovering at the far edge of the dome.

"They won't stay there long when they see Walker's dead," Paige said.

"Faster." And he leaned a hand on Paige's shoulder as he half hopped through the grass.

Chapter Fourteen

They approached the house warily, even though no one could have been there except perhaps Starky. After all, the ranger Collins was up prowling around in the helicopter, and the rest of the gang was disposed of. The original gang, that is. Were there new arrivals?

"Starky!" he called out as they approached the old house. There was no answer. "Starky!"

As he hobbled around the corner to the front of the house, David saw the fetid remains of Blinky, the pet condor, lying in the mud where it had been shot the day before. The carcass was crumpled not twenty feet from the end of the yellow wing of the airplane, its long chain still attached to the collar around its neck and the other end tied to a tree; in spite of the rain the flesh of the huge bird was swarming with flies and ants. A surge of new anger welled up inside of David at the senseless crime.

"Starky!" he called again.

There was still no answer. Had the little man been injured getting off the platform after the long slide? But if that had happened it would have occurred way over by the river, where the cable ended. Too far away and no time to look for him. David couldn't see the helicopter in the gray skies, but he could hear the sound of its blades.

He had been counting on Starky for some ingenious idea for defense or escape other than the crazy airplane attempt. He had run out of ideas himself and his shoulder wound throbbed and the pain in his knee was searing and the helicopter was not far off. He didn't want to leave Starky behind, but the little man would probably be safer on his own without them.

"The plane," he said simply.

Crouching, he led Paige under the wing to the fuselage, opened the door and helped her in.

As he hurried around to the pilot's side, hopping more than hobbling now, he looked up at the sound of the helicopter, but he could see nothing.

He threw away his crutch-stock and climbed in. It was hot in the plane, and smelled of gas fumes. He fastened his belt, slid open his window for air and stared at the instrument panel. Nothing about it looked familiar or intelligible. When he had learned to fly so long ago at the little Billings airfield the plane had been guided by a joystick, not a wheel, the throttle had been a lever beside the seat, not a knob jutting out at him near the altimeter, and a pilot needed another man to yank down on the propeller to start the motor. Among all the knobs and buttons and switches he saw the key protruding from the ignition plate. He turned it, and the propeller quivered, and revolved once and stopped. He remembered something about a chokelike knob that controlled the mix. There was a black knob near the ignition and he pulled it out part way.

He turned the key again, and the engine coughed and the propeller turned around twice before stopping. Then David pulled the big ivory-colored knob he assumed was the throttle out all the way and shoved it back in a little. He twisted the key, the prop whirled several times and with two loud backfires the engine caught and the prop kept turning. David worked the throttle and let the engine idle quietly.

He blew out a sigh. Jesus, he thought, maybe I *can* get this thing off the ground! But what then? He looked ahead at the end of the valley where the mountain crags were shrouded in rain clouds. Could he fly over them? And then could he remember enough, learn enough quickly enough about flying this plane, before running out of gas, to land it without killing them both? If there were any other choice he would never attempt it. But there was no other course and it was better to die in the attempt than to die like sitting ducks here.

The rain was beating down like hail on the wing over his head. He tried working the pedals back and forth to get the feel of the rudder, but the pain in his left knee was unbearable.

He pushed down on the right brake at the top of the pedal as hard as he could and at the same time shoved the throttle in all the way. The plane shuddered and rolled forward, tipping as it swung to the right.

In a moment the plane was bouncing over the field, gathering speed, the tires riding the soggy ground more easily when the fuselage grew lighter as the airstream traveled over the wings, the plane coming closer to being airborne.

Then suddenly he saw the stump of a cottonwood tree—a yard and a half high and partly hidden in the grass. He jammed his left foot on the pedal and yelled at the pain. The knee refused to hold his foot down on the control and the strut of the right wing snagged the stump.

There was a jolt, a ripping as the plane slammed violently to the left and slewed into the high grass with a crack. David heard and felt more than saw the yellow wing ripped off the fuselage, and the plane spun crazily around once as Paige cried out. When they lurched to a stop, David saw the helicopter drop down out of the dark sky above them.

"You all right?" he said.

"I think so," Paige moaned.

"Oh, God." He slammed his fist against the instrument panel. "Oh, God—we almost made it— so close, so close. . . ." He kept pounding the panel.

The helicopter was dropping below the tops of the trees and settling next to the plane, between David and Paige and the house. The bubble of glass was pushed open, and Collins, in his khaki ranger's uniform, heaved himself out of the aircraft. He was in no hurry—he knew he finally had his quarry.

"Out of the plane, Brand!"

David looked through the windshield and saw Collins walking toward them, shaking his head as though in sorrow. David quickly glanced around the plane for some kind of weapon. There was nothing but a small silver fire extinguisher held against the side of the cockpit by two clamps.

"Is that Starky over there?" asked Paige, point-ing.

David looked toward the house and thought he caught a glimpse of a form ducking around the trees.

"You're a fool, Brand!" called Collins as he came closer.

Now David could see the ranger's patch on the short-sleeved shirt, and the steel-rimmed glasses that caught the light in semaphore flashes.

David stealthily yanked the fire extinguisher from its clamps and put it between his feet.

"A damn fool," said Collins as he came up on David's side. The ranger's pistol was in its holster, and he leaned one hand against the fuselage. "And this mess is all of your own making."

"How do you—figure that, Collins?" David mumbled. He held his hand to his head as though he'd been badly hurt. But he looked under his fingers across Paige and and saw through her window that the pilot was not even bothering to leave the helicopter. He couldn't see Starky anywhere.

"All these deaths," said Collins in a regretful tone. "And now your deaths. And for what? A half a hundred prehistoric birds, that's for what. Birds that are on their way out anyway, as surely as the dinosaur. Birds no good to anyone."

"Thought it—was your—business, Collins—to protect wildlife," David said as though in pain. "Thought the government trusted you to take care of those birds—not help a bunch of thugs to kill them."

"Listen, you won't find anyone that cares more about wildlife than me," said Collins. "But do you think it's right that fifty-three thousand acres should be tied up just for forty-nine ugly birds? Acres where people could build huge dams for water and for energy. Like this valley here, perfect place for—"

"Oh, cut the crap! Kill us but cut the crap!"

He spotted Starky's figure stealing through the grass on the other side of the house. "How much did they pay you?"

"Pay me?"

"How much did the mine people, or dam people or whoever, pay you to help these killers eliminate the birds?" David could see Starky easing around a corner of the house now, behind the helicopter. "And which group paid all the money and furnished this helicopter and the plane for you to finish the job?"

"It doesn't matter who did. But I'll tell you, as long as you're so fuckin' curious and as long as it doesn't matter anymore, far as you're concerned."

He leaned forward, his eyes bright.

"Oil!" he hissed. "*Oil!* Every fuckin' foot of earth in this valley is soggy with oil! Oil for people, people's homes, people's cars. And if I got a little money—and I'm talkin' about peanuts—after all these years of working my ass off in a thankless job, that doesn't matter either! What matters is human beings! Hell, I'd like to protect *all* animals—condors and whales and baby seals or whatever. But we gotta protect the human animal first and foremost!"

"And we're not human beings?" said David, fighting for time. He could see that Starky had sneaked twenty feet behind the helicopter. But now he was kneeling down—doing what?

"We're not human beings—Paige and I? No right to live?"

Collins sighed. "I'm afraid you gave up that right. You traded that right for a bunch of birds that nobody needs anymore in this modern world."

David saw that Starky—incredibly—was doing nothing to help them. He was kneeling over his dead pet! He picked one hell of a time to bury the creature, if that's what he was doing.

"You'll save us all a lot of trouble," said Collins, holding out his hand. "The film."

"What film?" said David.

Collins put his face down close to the open window and David could see he was reaching for the gun in the holster.

"You know what film! I don't want anyone finding it after you've been disposed of."

"You mean the film I gave to the little man yesterday to keep for me?"

"You didn't give that film to no little man," Collins said between clenched teeth.

"You're right. I have it—I have it right here."

He leaned against the door, reached into his pocket and brought out the film cassette. He fumbled as he handed it towards Collins' out-stretched hand—and dropped it.

"There's your precious film."

Collins reached down to pick up the film from the grass. David grabbed the extinguisher and when Collins raised his head, David stabbed out with the metal cylinder, punching it as hard as he could into the ranger's face. The bottom of the cylinder rammed into the bridge of his nose, and he fell into the grass and sat there, holding his face with both hands as blood from his nostrils spurted through his fingers.

Quickly David opened the door and, reaching over, caught Paige by the wrist. He stepped out of the plane on his good leg and dragged Paige across the seat and out with him.

"This way!"

Leaning on her, he began stumbling through the grass toward the brush at the foot of the hills. It was a long way—probably half a mile. And the pilot would have seen Collins on the ground now, and the helicopter would surely get them before they could reach the cover. But it was better than sitting in the plane, waiting for them to burn it and them inside— or some other atrocity. A shot rang out.

He looked back as he ran and saw that it was the pilot firing. Collins was on his feet now and, holding his face with one hand, was moving toward the helicopter. The blades of the aircraft were already starting to turn as the pilot hauled Collins into the bubble.

"Can't go much further!" David gasped. "My knee!"

They reached a large log, and David fell behind it, pulling Paige down with him.

"Can't make it, Paige," he managed to say. "End of the line. They won't see me here. You go on."

"I'll stay with you."

"You go on!" he commanded.

"No."

The wet grass felt good and weariness flooded his body. He forced himself to lift his head and look over the log toward the house. The helicopter's blades were a blur now as it prepared to take off with the two men aboard. Suddenly David saw Starky run out behind the helicopter and tie something to a strut of the rear assembly near the tail rotor. At almost the same time the pilot lifted the aircraft off the ground.

The helicopter went straight up a dozen feet and then the pilot dropped the nose slightly, preparing to go forward. But suddenly the aircraft hit the end of the condor's chain, and though the chain snapped, the jerk tipped the helicopter, pulling it to the left. Before the pilot could right it, one of the blades caught the branch of a cottonwood tree. The aircraft tipped crazily on its side and a blade struck the ground as the pilot overcompensated. Then it cartwheeled directly toward Starky. David saw him make a running dive in an attempt to get out of its path, and the machine burst into a ball of flame as it hit the ground near the irrigation ditch.

After the terrible noise when it struck, there was a second explosion and then silence. A black cloud rose. There was no sign of life.

Paige began to sob.

"It's all right," said David, touching her hair. "We're safe now."

"And Maddy," Paige said finally. "Is she safe? And Starky? Is he safe?"

"I don't know—about Starky," he said, fighting to keep his voice from breaking. He lowered his head to the ground, and the wet grass felt cool on his eyes and forehead.

He thought of Maddy with a painful stab. Why did it have to turn out like that for her? What was that quote of Paige's grandfather? "Life is a practical joke, in the worst possible taste." And all this, as Collins had said, because of a few birds, forty-nine ugly birds.

He blew out a breath. He felt dizzy. I want to go back to Montana, he thought as he got up unsteadily. I haven't been there for a long time. Paige might like Montana—and I'll take Chris. But he knew that before he went anywhere there was an obligation to the remaining condors. The gang members who had died, and Collins—they were the tip of the iceberg—he would have to find out which oil company, which individuals, had hired Collins, and then get the *New York Times* or the *Washington...*

"David!" Paige cried jubilantly. "He's alive!"

The figure crawling out of the irrigation ditch was indeed Starky. Or something that resembled him. Even at this distance David could see that his hair and eyebrows had been burned off, and that his clothes were wet shreds hanging on his blackened body. The little man lurched over to the smoking corpse of the helicopter. He spat at its charred remains, then staggered completely around it once, spat again, stumbled and fell to his knees, his hands clasped in front of him.

David helped Paige up, put his arm around her and began hobbling toward Starky, who was back on his feet and walking slowly around the wreckage.

The rain had stopped, and as they walked, he looked out at the fields, the wet green fields, and here and there big circles of pale sun made yellow circus rings. He stared up at the skies, where ragged holes of blue were beginning to appear.

Up in those skies there were no condors in evidence now. Nor golden eagles nor redtailed hawks nor Cooper's hawks nor Harlan's hawks nor any other raptors. Only one small sparrow hawk that had started to work the field, hovering in one place by leaning back and rotating his wings fast, like a boy trying to keep his balance while falling off a fence; the bird had its neck arched and was looking down the length of its body, studying the terrain, waiting for the first little creature to venture out after the rain.

New Bestsellers from Berkley
The best in paperback reading

___ **IMPERIAL NIGHTS**   04233-2—$2.50
Olivia O'Neill
___ **THE LAST CONVERTIBLE**   04034-8—$2.50
Anton Myrer
___ **LEAH'S JOURNEY**   04430-0—$2.50
Gloria Goldreich
___ **THE LEGACY**   04183-2—$2.25
John Coyne, based on a story by Jimmy Sangster
___ **MOMMIE DEAREST**   04444-0—$2.75
Christina Crawford
___ **NIELSEN'S CHILDREN**   04111-5—$2.50
James Brady
___ **NO BED OF ROSES**   04241-3—$2.50
Joan Fontaine
___ **NURSE**   04220-0—$2.50
Peggy Anderson
___ **PURSUIT**   04258-8—$2.50
Robert L. Fish
___ **THE SIXTH COMMANDMENT** 04271-5—$2.75
Lawrence Sanders